Fire on the Ramparts

Book Two

Sugar Hill Series

By M.L. Bullock

Dedication

This book is dedicated to my children who allowed me to practice my storytelling skills every night at bedtime.

Shh! Did you hear footsteps in the hallway?

He would not stay for me, and who can wonder?
He would not stay for me to stand and gaze.
I shook his hand, and tore my heart in sunder,
And went with half my life about my ways.

A. E. Houseman

1859-1936

Prologue – Susanna Serene Dufresne

The Ramparts 1821

My legs wobbled beneath me, but I couldn't stop now. Shawntee's heavy footsteps stomped behind me, and I imagined I could feel his breathing. It was hard and heavy, like his fists. Hoping to lose him in the crowded streets and twisting alleyways of the Ramparts, I turned and turned again. I did not dare look behind me—I did not want to see his ferocious snarl. The dark-skinned man's eyes were like a wolf's—narrow and green and absent of any humanity or compassion. All of Etienne's daughters knew that when Shawntee turned those eyes upon you, you were doomed. Flower knew this.

And Genevieve. Poor Genevieve.

How many of Etienne's "daughters" had he demanded favors from? How many had suffered his wrath when they refused? For all her careful words about the importance of virtue, Etienne failed to protect us from her own brother.

Oh God, don't let him kill me.

It rained hard tonight, and the stones were slick and cold under my feet—I could feel the sliminess beneath my shoes. These shoes were meant for indoor activities, not running through the Ramparts. I tripped through a pile of refuse that littered Poor Man's Lane, but I could not stop! I would run through hell itself if I had to! I sobbed as I struggled to stay on my weak legs.

How had this happened to me? I was the wife of Chase Dufresne! I had received no papers of divorce, and no solicitor had come to notify me that Chase and I were no longer married. I would not take Etienne's word alone. I would see my husband myself, and then I would know the truth. Yes, then I would know what to do. If he wanted to divorce me, he must tell me so himself.

Please, Chase. Please help me!

Despite his abandonment these many months, I could not make myself believe he had cast me off forever. I had been a fool, but surely I had paid for my sins.

Shawntee growled my name. *Susanna!*

His deep voice rang menacingly through the alleyway, and no one was there to help me. I looked left and then right, wiping the rain from my face. I felt the blood on the insides of my legs, but there was nothing I could do about that now. I had to escape!

Etienne had stolen my baby—and left me to die! I had to believe my daughter lived—yes, she must live because Etienne needed her. She would need to recoup the losses she imagined I had caused her. I had not been allowed to see my daughter's face, yet I imagined it. I had cried and begged Etienne before I passed out to allow me to hold the baby just once, but when I awoke to my cold, empty room, both she and my baby were gone.

She had what she wanted—her payment for my marriage. I had cried and screamed, but no one came. Sulli's warning had echoed in my ears, reminding me of what would happen to me if I remained here. I had managed to dress myself and slowly creep down the stairs. Surprisingly, no one was downstairs either.

Was it Sunday? Yes, it was, and all the house was at Mass for a little while. I knew it was my chance— probably my only chance!

What of the curse? What of Sulli's charm? I did not want to believe that Sulli's charm would unintentionally work against my baby or me, but I knew her magic was strong. Had it ever missed its mark? I'd been laboring for two days, and there'd been no sign of Sulli. Etienne must have forbidden her entrance. Why else would she, my true mother, not help me?

I've lost my mother and my daughter!

"Stop, Susanna! Stop right now!" The voice did not sound like Shawntee's, but I dared not answer it.

I scrambled in front of a carriage, waving my hands frantically trying to force the driver to stop, but he did not. I briefly tripped over my skirts but got up again. If I stayed in the mud, I would stay down forever. This was the moment, the moment that counted. I would look back on this moment one day and say, "Yes, everything changed then. Right then." I had no tears, my voice was gone and I was emotionally and physically spent, but I would fight on. I got back on my feet and looked for a way to escape. And which way should I go? How much farther could I run?

Shawntee was on the other side of the street now, waiting for the carriages to pass by. His evil glare told me that he would not only catch me but hurt me in crueler ways than I could imagine. "Someone help me!" I screamed at the carriages that rode up and down. To my utter surprise, a black carriage stopped, and I caught my breath. The carriage had a gold "D" painted on the door panel, and I knew whose it was—this was a Dufresne carriage!

I ran to the door and stood on the side of the carriage. I was sure I looked a sight, but Chase would have mercy on me. He would have to help me—if he ever loved me, he would have to!

"Please..." I began my plea.

"Get in," the figure said from the darkness of the carriage as he flung open the door. Without question, I obeyed and leaned back against the seat with my eyes closed as I tried to catch my breath.

Yes, Shawntee. Go tell your sister that I have gone home to be with my Chase—we will be free now, free from your grasp.

We had at last satisfied her evil terms. She had our daughter as payment! And I heard that Arthur Dufresne was dead. What could keep us apart?

Then, as if Fate intended to answer me, a shaft of moonlight revealed the face of my rescuer. It was not my own dear husband, Chase. My breath stilled as I stared into the face of my betrayer, the one who had wrought all this agony upon me. *Ambrose.* It was he who had bade me pledge to be his soul mate, not for this life alone but for all the lives after it. He who had seduced me and left me nude and vulnerable on the tiny island in the pond beside Sugar Hill.

My skin was already freezing, but now my blood ran cold too. A curl of cigarette smoke wafted between us, and he leaned back in the corner of the coach. His elegantly shod foot rested on the seat beside him, his elbow on his knee as he observed me. It was as if he did not know quite what to do with me. As if I were something repugnant he'd discovered on the bottom of his shoe.

Perhaps he would finally kill me and end the agony of my hopeless life. Perhaps he would. But couldn't he have done that already? How many times had I seen him walk past the window of my prison? More than a few months. Usually he did not acknowledge me, yet other times he was mockingly polite and raised his hat or cast his wide smile at me. Beyond that, he did not come to see me or offer me any help whatsoever. Now he was here, my soul mate, my torturer, the man who'd brought me to ruin.

And there was nowhere left to run.

I heard a loud sound, a rock striking the side of the carriage. I nearly screamed, and Ambrose stared at me, his dark eyes appraising me, his full red lips keeping the cigarette in place. The carriage came to a stop at a street crossing, and the driver let out a yelp of disgust. To my surprise Shawntee ran to the door of the carriage and swung it open. In a gruff voice he commanded, "Get out, Susanna. Come out and leave the nice man alone. You wouldn't want to get him hurt."

At that, Ambrose flicked out his cigarette through the opposite window and without so much as a word kicked Shawntee in the face with the bottom of his black boot, sending the tall man sprawling to the ground. Shawntee screamed like he'd been shot, but his pain didn't move Ambrose. He reached in his pocket and removed a few coins, tossed them out the window at Shawntee, closed the door and then slapped the side of the carriage. Etienne's brother did not come after us again. The last glance I had of him, he was picking up the coins and stuffing them in his pockets. He stared at us but did not make any effort to continue his pursuit. I didn't know what Ambrose might be thinking, but I knew Shawntee well enough to know he'd try again. Eventually.

Ambrose was elegantly dressed as he always was, but I appeared as if I had been walking the streets of the Ramparts all night. And if Etienne had had her way, I would have been. She had no love in her. No mercy. What a fool I had been all these years to think she cared for me as a mother loved a daughter.

And still Ambrose said nothing, but at least now those dark eyes were fixed on the countryside and not on me. I began to worry about where he was taking me. This road would not lead us to Sugar Hill; where was I bound?

"Are you taking me back to Chase? This is not the way to Sugar Hill."

"Oh, the things you say, Susannah. As if I would be a party to bigamy." He clucked his tongue at me as if I were the silliest woman he'd ever spoken to.

"Bigamy? What do you mean? I have married no one else!"

"Ah, that may be true, or it may not be true, but for sure Chase has married Athena Pelham. And they are expecting a son. He does not wish to see you. You are an adulteress, Susanna Serene. There is no changing that."

Despite his rescue of me I lashed out at him, "And I have you to thank for that, with your pretty words! Everything you said was a lie! You tricked me and abandoned me, Ambrose. You left me to face it all on my own." I was weeping furiously now. "Let me out now! I would rather die than stay in your company. You have brought me nothing but misfortune for all your words."

He gripped my wrists, pulled me close to him and whispered in my ear, "Why should I let you go? We made a pledge to one another, Susanna! There is no going back! Did you think there wouldn't be a price to be paid?" He released my wrists, and I rubbed them to ease the pain. I knew that his rough handling would leave bruises on my skin. "You will remain with me at Thorn Hill."

I blinked at him, scarcely believing his words. "I cannot believe you would think I would consent to go anywhere with you. I do not want to be with you. I would never agree to that. So unless you want to force yourself upon me..."

He tossed back his head and laughed at that. "My dear, in your current state you are hardly a seductive morsel. Far from the Belle of the Quadroon Ball now. Fortunately for you, we have a bond that cannot be broken, dear Susanna Serene. And I don't think I'll need to go to those extremes. For all the hate you have for me now, one day you will desire me again. I am confident of that." He dug in his black and gray suit pocket and found another cigarette.

I had no words after hearing such a ridiculous declaration, so he continued, "You see the smaller picture. I see the larger picture; I have rid us of an obstacle—

the obstacle of your unfortunate and unhappy marriage. Now that you have made peace with that bitch, Etienne, we can move on with our own lives, our own plans."

"Plans? What plans? You must be mad! I do not want to be with you, Ambrose. I love Chase—I will always love him! I will make him see this was all a mistake." Then inspiration struck me. Ambrose could make this all go away if he were only willing to tell my husband the truth. Perhaps he would, if he truly loved me. I reached across the bench and touched his hand. "Show me that you are a man of honor, Ambrose. Tell Chase the truth about us, that you betrayed me to take your vengeance on him!"

With steely anger, Ambrose banged on the side of the carriage again, opened the door and stepped outside. "Is that what you think? That I wanted vengeance? I told you who we were and what we were. I did not make you do anything you didn't wish to do, Susanna!" The carriage had stopped on a long, dark road. I blinked at him in the darkness. I did not know where we were, but I was still freezing and now even more frightened. I was sure Ambrose would throw me out of his carriage. Instead he walked to the front and spoke to the driver. In a minute, he came back and spoke less kindly now.

"Go see for yourself, Susanna Serene. Go to Sugar Hill and see what awaits you there. You are a fool! However, if you do go, know that I will never forgive you.

If you reject me now, I will make sure you pay for any affection you receive from me later." I could hardly understand what he meant by that threat, but his refusal to help me with Chase angered me.

"I will never have any affection toward you, Ambrose. Let me go!"

With a dark look he jumped up and stood in the carriage doorway. "Then so be it. And when you are finished making a fool of yourself, *my soul mate,* come to Thorn Hill. When you do return, never will his name pass your lips—in my presence or out of it!"

Suddenly, Ambrose kissed me savagely, and then without another word he was gone. *This surely must be some kind of cruel trick. What is happening?* As always, Ambrose confused me. I poked my head out of the window as we drove away. Ambrose walked in the other direction, presumably toward Thorn Hill, and he'd already lit another cigarette.

I curled up in the seat and after a little while fell asleep in the carriage, uncaring about my stained skirts, my unkempt hair, my swollen red eyes and bare, dirty feet. All I wanted was my own dear love, my Chase, my husband! He would have to hear the truth—he would have to know that I loved him still. When I woke up, the carriage had stopped. Through the Spanish-moss-covered oak trees I could see the bright lights of the house that I had once thought of as my prison. Now I wanted nothing more than to go back there. I could endure anything, even a spirit's taunts, to be with Chase again. Was I dreaming? Could this really be true? After a few seconds of hesitation I reasoned that I could not linger here in the carriage forever.

My hands and feet were dirty, and one sleeve of my dress was torn. I pinched my cheeks to give my face some much-needed color and rubbed my lips furiously in an attempt to make them look healthy and desirable. My stomach cramped, and I took a deep breath against the pain. I twisted my hair into a loose braid and let it hang over my shoulder. I looked like a strumpet, but I defiantly thought, "Let him see how he'd left me!"

I stepped out of the carriage and walked up the steps on wobbly legs. It sounded as if there were a party inside, a celebration of some kind. I shouldn't go in, but what choice did I have? I had to see him—I had dreamed of this moment for so long!

Still, my inner voice advised caution, and before walking inside I called to the driver, "Do not leave until I've dismissed you." He begrudgingly agreed, and I walked onto the porch and into the house. I did not tap on the door knocker or wait to be announced. I walked in as if I were still mistress at Sugar Hill.

Iona saw me first. She was walking into the house from the open back door, carrying a tray of boiled shrimp, sliced lemons and salt. Her eyes widened when she saw me, and I thought she would drop her tray, but I raced past the closed dining room door and caught her before she stumbled. "Miss Susanna, you ain't supposed to be here. I thought you were dead. They told us you were dead! Oh God!"

"No, Iona. I am not a ghost. It is really me." I hugged her, but she stiffened under my embrace. No, she was not happy to see me, although I believed she had genuine affection for me. "Let me have the tray. I will take it in."

"Oh no! That would never do. He is not alone. His other—I mean to say, he's not by himself, Miss Susanna."

"I have never asked you for anything, Iona. Please let me do this. Let me carry the tray in. He will not punish you. I swear it." She must have felt pity for me because she agreed, despite her misgivings. And what could she do? Technically I was still Mrs. Dufresne, wasn't I? Or at least one of them.

"It's going to be bad if you go in there, miss. Don't go in there. He's not the same."

I touched her face and stared into her frightened eyes. "None of us are. Let me through, Iona." I tossed my hair behind my back and raised my chin. I wanted to see Chase, and if this was the only way, so be it. I was tired of being his secret sin! He would see me— and so would his friends and his new wife!

I took a deep breath and walked in with the tray of food. At first, no one addressed me. Chase entertained six couples, men in stiff collars and women dressed in fine silks, just as I used to do. When they broke from their various activities and deigned to notice me, they looked shocked. The golden candelabras were lit on the shiny wooden tables where the couples were playing cards and drinking. A petite woman with red hair and extremely pale skin hovered near Chase. She whispered in his ear and pointed at the cards he held in his hand. It was an intimate moment, and it broke my heart to see it. By the way she kissed his cheek, I gathered this was the new Mrs. Dufresne.

And yes. She knew me too.

Then everything stopped. Chase's light blue eyes fell on me while everyone else watched to see how he would respond to my invasion. Yes, they would know me. Surely they'd heard rumors about me. I could almost hear their whispers.

That's Chase Dufresne's mulatto woman. His sinful indulgence. His forgotten whore.

Athena touched his shoulder and looked at him questioningly, but he did not answer her. He rose from the table, his face unreadable as he came toward me. Feeling weak now, I nearly dropped the tray. A few boiled shrimp fell off the silver platter and hit the ground. I felt myself fainting, yet I could hear the others whispering behind me.

"Susanna…"

"Chase…I…"

"Susanna, come out here," he said, but there was no love in his voice. It was an empty, wooden sound. I knew there was no hope for me. And none for my daughter. He would not help us. Chase took the tray from me and placed it on the buffet table. "My friends, please excuse me."

"Chase?" Athena whispered.

Chase gripped my elbow and forcibly propelled me toward the door.

"No! I want them to see me! You can't just forget me!" I stammered foolishly at him. "I am your wife, Chase!" His face was unmoving, like granite. The redheaded woman had a wretched look on her face. She was not a great beauty, not at all. Her forehead was large and her green eyes even larger. She was petite but fierce looking, like a wild forest creature. I believed she would kill me if she could.

"Chase, please, listen to me. I have to speak with you," I pleaded with him. "Please, we must talk. Etienne, she has our daughter. You cannot abandon us!" He did not answer me, but I felt his heavy breathing. He was practically dragging me down the hallway now. I cried and fell on the plush burgundy carpet. Without mercy he snatched me up by my shoulders and continued pushing me to the door.

The party tumbled out into the hallway to watch how my husband would deal with me.

"Chase! Stop, please!"

No, there was no trace of the man I once loved. He was gone. I had burned out the love he had for me as one would snuff out a candle. And that was the agony of it all—I had done this.

A servant flitted in front of us. "Open the door," he commanded him. We were only a few steps away now.

"No, Chase. Our daughter! She needs us! Help me find her! Despite what you think about me, you must help our daughter. Please!"

Finally he spun me about and peered into my soul with murderous eyes. "Madam, you are not in control of your mental faculties. Our daughter, if she *is* mine, is dead. I don't know what game you are playing. What did you think you would accomplish by coming here? I do not want you here, Susanna." The ferocity of his words would brand my soul forever. "Now leave. Do not come back, unless you wish to serve as a slave in this house."

I gasped. "You cannot mean this?"

"As far as I am concerned, you are dead. Do not return."

"Why won't you believe me? Ambrose betrayed me—he betrayed us both. I know that now. Please, my husband. Do not send me away!"

With one mighty shove he pushed me out the door, and I fell in a heap on the porch. I wept and begged him to speak to me. He did not immediately leave but said nothing for a long time. It felt like forever, and I was in misery. If only I could will myself to die! I could die with my daughter. Then maybe we could be together, for I would rather be with her than live without her and without the love of her father.

"You *will not* return here. You *are not* my wife. The only reason I have not served you divorce papers is because...I understand what that will mean for you. Despite your shortcomings, I do not want that. I loved you once," he whispered as if the thought repulsed him, "but if you return I will not hesitate to do just that. I never want to see you again." I could not bear the expression of disgust on his face. I watched his shiny black shoes as he went back into the house. The heavy door closed between us, and I was left on the dimly lit porch with the dogs.

I could not have imagined this. What to do now?

I felt weaker by the minute, and I was certain I had a fever. For the second time tonight I pulled myself out of the mud and walked like a soulless corpse to the carriage. I didn't think about my destination. I allowed Fate and the carriage to decide for me. Wherever it stopped was where I would disembark. And then I would find somewhere to die. What was there to live for?

I closed the curtains and lay on the seat, and soon I fell asleep.

When I woke again Ambrose was there. I was inside Thorn Hill, I assumed. The blue painted bedroom was filled with a ridiculous number of candles. The place seemed more like a chapel than a bedroom. Yes, I certainly had a fever now, and blood was pouring even more freely down my thighs. How much blood could I have left? Perhaps I would bleed to death! Busy hands patted my thighs, and as I pushed them away I screamed, "Let me die! Let me bleed!" I passed out and woke to just a few burning candles. The room was dim. Someone was near.

Sulli? Mother? Is that you?

It was not Sulli but Ambrose and a dark-skinned doctor who clucked and fussed over me.

Ambrose's face revealed no emotion as he watched the other man attend to my injuries. The strange little man placed cool cloths on my forehead and examined my eyes. "Now behave yourself, so we gwan get you better. You's fever is gone, but it is God's wonder you not dead." His voice was soothing. I recognized him from somewhere—yes, I'd seen him at the Quadroon Ball.

Ambrose smoked his cigarette in the corner of the room. He watched the doctor's ministrations as if I were some sort of specimen, a butterfly he would like to add to his collection. I watched him too. How aloof he was; as always his face revealed nothing. And he had been right. I had been a fool. Twice the fool. Wasn't that the beginning of a poem?

For a moment I was back in the gazebo, watching myself make the choice that would change my life. I had spoken the words. They could not be unspoken. Sulli's magic sealed me to my fate. Yes, I had wrought this with my silly heart. And by doing so, I had consigned myself to eternal misery. All hope of reconciliation with Chase vanished in that moment. I would no longer be a fool for love, for it had taken me low—lower than I'd ever imagined.

Ambrose had warned me what it would mean if I rejected him. What torments now awaited me?

Yes, I tumbled into the deepest pit of despair, where no light shined and no relief would find me. This was where I would dwell. I would never love again, and I would forever dwell in this pit.

But somehow I would find a way to bring Chase and Ambrose down with me.

PART ONE

Chapter One – Avery Dufresne

Dufresne board meetings were refreshingly different from any meeting I attended at News Quarter. The offices weren't in a glass skyscraper but in a wide, brick building quite by itself. They weren't located in a commercial complex but rather tucked away off Hickory Lane on a rounded hill. If there weren't so many pecan trees in the way, I could have very easily seen Sugar Hill from here. With the coming of fall, most of the trees in the county were bare, except for a few lonely pines and other evergreens. There was a wooden sign on the front of the building that read "D & D Properties," but there was nothing else to identify who and what we were. I doubted that even the locals would know what was happening here. And how could they know? Dufresnes didn't flaunt our money, but we did put it to good use.

As matrone, the symbolic CEO of our family fortune, that was my purpose—do good things for as many people as possible. So the humble building suited us just fine.

Inside was no different; there were no ostentatious chandeliers or spiral staircases, not like what you would see at Sugar Hill. According to Reed, the small office complex was built in 1975. There had been a much lovelier older building here, he said, but it burnt to the ground in 1974 and this was put up in its place. It was a comfortable place with wooden paneling and fantastic mahogany and cedar furniture. I loved the smell of it. It smelled like tradition. So different from my corner office on floor seven of the News Quarter building. There it smelled of nothing except expensive coffee and a mixture of colognes and perfumes, the scents of the affluent who called NQ their work-home.

As always when we arrived at the board's building, Minnie Dufresne met us at the reception desk. The young woman had dark blond hair, almond-shaped brown eyes and honey-colored skin. She had a tendency to speak slowly, but she was not unintelligent; she was very careful with her words.

She smiled politely at me as she handled phone calls and inquiries. We did not chitchat today. Maybe after the meeting, if we got out of here at a decent time, I would have the opportunity to catch up with her. I had no idea what else she did, but she was obviously a lovely young lady. It was such a relief to be here and not at the NQ building.

There were no shiny anchormen and women here. No fake smiles and hidden knives. No hidden ambition and secret plans for mergers and takeovers.

No cold-hearted backstabbers or murderers here.

This was my family, and these were real salt-of-the-earth people. For all their net worth, they didn't strut around or flash their money. The Dufresnes seemed comfortable with their wealth, and that was so diametrically opposed to my former life, where being the alpha was all that mattered. For the first time in my life, I felt as if I belonged somewhere. For the life of me I could not understand why Vertie wanted to keep me away from all these friendly faces. It seemed so out of character. Reed had no official information to offer me on the subject, and Summer swore she didn't remember ever meeting Vertie. She suggested I ask Mitchell. I had not quite worked up the courage to quiz my shy cousin because I desperately wanted to make him my friend. I got the distinct impression that pushing him to talk would only push him away. But if Miss Anne valued him and treated him as her second-in-command, shouldn't I at least consider doing the same?

I smiled as I watched Reed work the room. Of all the Dufresne men, he was the most handsome—no, beautiful would be a better word for him. Not in a feminine way but exceptionally handsome, of that there was no doubt. He dressed impeccably and even now, with his suit jacket folded neatly over the back of a vacant chair and the cuffs of his crisp white shirt rolled up, he looked like a man who could easily star in a cologne commercial. He caught me staring and grinned flirtatiously at me. I tried to pretend I didn't see that. We were cousins, for goodness' sake! We couldn't "hook up" or whatever you called it down here in Alabama. That would be too weird, even if he was a beautiful hunk of a man.

"Good Lord, calm your hormones," I whispered to myself. Suddenly as if she knew what I was saying, a voice beside me said, "I don't blame you. If I were thirty years younger, I'd be on him like white on rice."

"What?" An embarrassed laugh escaped my lips.

"We all think he's gorgeous. There's nothing to be ashamed of. He's a man and you are a woman. It's not unusual for cousins to be attracted to one another, especially in our family when the name means so much. And the bloodline."

"No, Pepper, I wasn't saying that I was ashamed. I mean..."

She snapped her gum and grinned. "Okay." She tossed her gum in the garbage can, ignored the receptionist and walked into the boardroom, leaving me behind.

As a newscaster I had covered many stories about family pride, family perseverance, the enduring love and strength of familial ties. It had always been a powerful thing to hear, but I didn't quite understand it until I experienced it myself. Since my "return" I felt as if I'd gotten a fair dose of it. Even Pepper, as blunt and in your face as she was—I respected and valued her too. She was family!

I had family members show up with homemade baked goods every week. Once a week, Dufresne men volunteered to do repairs on Sugar Hill, and one morning a group of Dufresne women showed up to dust the library. It was a strange and wonderful thing to experience. Summer always reminded me I could tell them no, but how could I?

"Suit yourself," she'd said. "But one day you'll want to. And if you wait, you'll hurt their feelings. Don't let them get into a habit of doing all these things for you, or else they may make you feel as if you owe them somehow. And you don't owe them a thing." I ignored her advice and kept my mouth shut, accepting all their help, their gifts of time and service. It was a humbling thing for sure.

Next week marked my three-month anniversary. Yes, I'd been at Sugar Hill for three whole months. In that short time I'd gotten quite close to many in my family, including little Dolly Jane, her family, Reed and Summer. Even Mitchell had begun to come around now, occasionally leaving the comfort of Miss Anne's Rose Cottage to visit me. He didn't say much at first, and I often felt as if he *wanted* to say something but never did. Mitchell was kind and frequently looked for little tasks to do for me, like prune the roses or walk the brown and white spaniel that showed up in my house one day.

And then there was the house.

It was hardly just a house. It was like a living museum that never gave tours. And maybe we *should* give tours a few times a year. I would love to see others enjoying the Angel Gallery and hear music playing in the gazebo. I would love to see children playing on the Great Lawn.

Funny how that worked out. The very things I wanted with Jonah, the white picket fence experience, going to church and working in the garden—all that had come true. Seriously, that argument all those months ago almost seemed prophetic now. Only Jonah had not been a part of the plan.

As much as I loved the family, I also loved Sugar Hill. It was more than just an old house. Every corner held an important artifact, a glimpse into my newly discovered past. And since the ghosts had vanished, or at least quieted down, I felt much safer in the grand old place.

Reed broke into my quiet contemplation as he took on his *I'm-the-boss voice* and said, "Everyone take a few minutes to read over the reports. Let me know if you have any questions." He slid the last stack of papers to me, and like my fellow board members I flipped through the sheets. This was my third board meeting, and so far I had no questions at all, except maybe, *How in the heck did the Dufresne clan come up with this kind of cash?* Of course, it seemed very uncouth to ask such a thing, so I didn't. I swallowed as my eyes fell on the final page. Even three months in, the numbers staggered my imagination. Was I really responsible for overseeing this kind of capital? I gave the report a perfunctory flip-through and waited for everyone else to do the same.

Officially there were twelve board members. I was the thirteenth person in the room; I wasn't on the board, but I was the deciding vote in any ties. For the board to operate and vote on anything, only six board members had to attend, but everyone was allowed a vote and could call them in. Then the votes were counted to decide the yea or nay. It was a simple system. I didn't interfere much, and so far I had not been asked to break any ties, until now. I might make history today.

Over the past three months I'd met all twelve members except Caspar Dufresne, who had to resign due to illness. At the last meeting we reviewed nominations for new board members, and to my surprise the process was quite contentious. Nobody could agree on a single name, and in the end Reed dismissed us to "think about it reasonably." It hadn't helped. After a quick solicitation for nominees at the beginning of this meeting and a few other votes on minor things, we'd once again been given a break, this time for lunch and a review of the previous nominees. Nobody had any questions concerning the finances, but everyone except me had an opinion about who should take Caspar's coveted spot. Apparently, on a Dufresne board, you served for life.

"Let's take up the nominations again, but please keep in mind that we will not leave this room today without having come to a consensus. We are family. We must put the needs of our family ahead of our own personal desires. That's just the way it is. I hope you will agree with me." Of course, everyone expressed that agreement with polite clapping, and Reed continued with a gentler tone, "The new quarter begins next week. Without all the board signing off, we can't approve a budget. But we can't do that without a new board member. We've got important things coming up, like Dolly Jane's surgery and the Dufresne-Wyncott Project."

"And the consideration for the Starlight Foundation," I added as I raised my hand.

"Yes, that too," Reed said. "So please, what can we do to come to some agreement? I still have three nominees here. I have committed votes from those who are absent, but each nominee has four votes. It's hard for me to believe we remain this divided. Now who's willing to give here?"

Pepper spoke first. She was an older woman with jet-black hair and a penchant for costume jewelry. "I stand by my nomination for Alexander James. Yes, he's my son, but he's a brilliant accountant with more degrees than most of us here put together."

"And he's your son," Danforth retorted angrily.

"I do believe I said that," Pepper snapped back.

"I just wanted to make that plain to everyone." Danforth rarely spoke, but when he did, it was usually something negative. Why was this guy always angry? Short with thick spectacles and a definitive

Southern accent, Danforth didn't mind sharing his thoughts with the board.

"I resent your insinuation."

Before they could begin arguing again, Reed interrupted, "No extraneous commentary, please. Who else renews their previous nomination?"

As it turned out, there had been no changes of heart. None at all. That was bad news for me. The same three individuals were put forward again, and again the group squabbled over which of the three would get the spot. This was a problem as Jamie was in town and time was ticking away. After listening to about thirty minutes more of the back-and-forth, inspiration hit me.

"What about Mitchell?" I asked between sniping. "What's wrong with him? He's quick and intelligent, and he was devoted to Miss Anne. It probably wouldn't take much to get him caught up on all the pending business."

Reed stared at me and smiled. "Yes, I agree." Nobody spoke, no one argued. I could see the gathering pondering my proposal. One by one, they slowly agreed. "So that's seven. With you included, Avery. That's all we need, but with your permission, I'll call the other board members and give them a chance to make their preference known. For the record."

"Don't bother. Nobody is going to go against the matrone." Pepper gave me a look, and that got my dander up. Her statement more than perturbed me.

"What does that mean? I hope that's not true. This isn't a monarchy, Pepper. It was merely a suggestion."

"And a damn good one," Danforth said, standing and stretching his back. "Can we go now? My show is coming on in thirty minutes, and I promised Margie I'd stop to pick up her beer."

The other members rose, including Pepper, who stalked to the notebook and officially wrote Mitchell's name on the page. Apparently this was also a tradition. Who came up with that idea? So much tradition in the Dufresne clan. And like any other family, we had our disagreements. None of us were perfect—certainly not me. I was willing to let bygones be bygones, if Pepper was.

All the others signed the book too, including Danforth, Elizabeth Page, Brian (whom everyone called Brian Senior) and finally Reed. With some irritation I watched the others exit; Reed hung back and stuffed his papers in his briefcase.

"Did I miss something? Why the hostility from Pepper?"

"Well, can you blame her?"

I picked up my purse and followed him to the door as he turned off the light. "What do you mean?"

He smiled at me, and it had a touch of sadness to it. Or was that just evidence that his patience was wearing thin? He'd been a fount of information during my first ninety days here, but he was noticeably more withdrawn lately. I couldn't account for it. And to think, a few minutes ago I was thinking how lucky I was to be a Dufresne. And how damn fine he was.

"She could hardly go against the matrone, could she?"

"What's wrong with Mitchell? If he wasn't a good nominee, you should have said something."

"Avery," he said as we walked toward the parking lot, "you have a lot of influence. Be careful how you wield it. If I were you, I'd limit your input to making project suggestions and casting tie-breaking votes. If you don't, you might find yourself with a bit more resistance than you are accustomed to."

"I don't get your meaning." I was still stymied, but I got the idea he wasn't pleased with me.

"I mean, it's been easy for you so far, thanks in part to Aunt Anne, who took care of much of the pressing business before she died. Now, that's really all the advice I have to give you. I have to head home too. Look, don't worry. I know you'll do just fine. And for the record, Mitchell was the right choice."

"Great. Well, thanks for that."

"Oh, one more thing. I meant to mention this earlier. There is a paranormal team from My Haunted Plantation scheduled to stop by Sugar Hill. Have you seen that television show?"

"What? No, of course not."

"Apparently Aunt Anne contacted them before she died, even signed an agreement allowing them permission to explore the premises. You'll have to play hostess; my apologies about that. I'm sure Summer will help you keep them corralled into whatever rooms you find suitable. The MHP team, as they like to call themselves, are to tour Sugar Hill and Thorn Hill, and maybe the grounds. But look on the bright side, it's probably good for public relations. People like the idea of haunted houses. Might help us somewhere down the line."

"This is wildly inconvenient, Reed. What am I supposed to do, let a bunch of strangers tromp through the house? Who are these people? Freaks? Weirdos? Oh my God! They aren't doing any séances here, are they?"

"No, absolutely not. They have been given strict instructions about that."

"I can't believe that Miss Anne would have agreed to this."

Hitting his fob to unlock his door, Reed pitched his briefcase in the passenger seat. "Well, she did. I have the contract. Would you like to see it?"

Again with the hostility?

"I'll take your word for it. You haven't led me wrong so far. I trust you, Reed, to continue leading me in the right direction. I'm sure I'll get it wrong a hundred more times."

"I doubt that. You're a quick study, Avery Dufresne." He shook his head and avoided my eyes. That was also strange. My cousin had always been one to look you in the eye, to give you his full attention. I couldn't understand what had changed. Whatever clouds crossed his mind, he soon forgot them because he squeezed my hand and flashed his Hollywood smile at me.

"You know, if you want to avoid the ghost hunters, you could always go stay at Thorn Hill. It's beautifully kept. It's much smaller than the big house, but it is very comfortable and perfect for entertaining guests. You know, like your friend from up north."

Oh. So that's it. Reed didn't approve of Jamie. What should I say? Should I say anything? I decided against it. It really wasn't any of his business, was it? I certainly didn't tell *him* who he should date. We had nothing going, except I began to suspect that he found me as attractive as I found him. Best to move on quickly from thoughts like that.

"Maybe I will do that. I haven't even visited Thorn Hill yet, and I have been meaning to. Sounds like a good idea. Well, take care." I walked toward my car as he got in his. Before he drove off and while I fumbled with my phone in the driver's seat, he pulled up beside me and rolled down his window. I hit the button to end my call to Jamie and rolled down mine.

"Be careful, Avery. Take care of yourself. We're all depending on you to lead our family into the future."

"Okay, well, no pressure there, huh?"

With an enigmatic grin he eased his car away and turned onto the road.

I watched his car lights disappear down the road and pulled out behind him. For some reason I had the sudden urge to turn the car around and drive back to Atlanta.

Maybe I should have.

Chapter Two – Jamie Richards

My ex-wife left me a string of vicious voicemails, but I didn't bother listening to a single one of them. I wasn't late on the house note, and thankfully we didn't have any children together, so no worries about buying diapers or paying into the college fund. That had been another disappointment in our marriage. But as it turned out, it had been a blessing in disguise.

I'd lost my bulldog in the divorce, but there wasn't a damn thing I could do about it. Evelyn fought like heck to keep him, even though she didn't even like him. In the end, the judge fell for those long, fluttering eyelashes and her sexy figure. For him to believe anything that came out of her mouth...it showed he was a complete fool. So she got the dog. I could have visitation, if I agreed to her terms. According to Evelyn, that meant going to my own house, the one I was paying for, on scheduled days. Drinking wine with her. Letting her toy with my emotions and whatever else she liked and then kick me out. As much as I loved Buddy, and I loved that dog better than most people, I could not ever put myself through that again.

Needless to say, seeing Atlanta disappear in my rearview mirror again gave me quite a bit of relief. I hadn't been able to break away for almost a month, and I had a growing desire to see Avery. Yes, I needed this. I didn't want to rush things, but I couldn't help but fantasize about us—together, naked and alone. Avery was exciting, confident and extremely attractive. But more than that, she was strong. Despite her perfectly feminine appearance, she had hidden strength. The kind that kept you alive, no matter what. I admired that. She'd survived an attack so vicious that it would have killed most. I'd seen those kinds of crime scenes firsthand. They stay with you. Forever.

And it wasn't the first time she survived death. I'd researched her background while working her case, and her past was littered with near misses. Her parents had been killed by a freak accident—stonework fell off a building and crashed onto their car, killing them instantly. What were the odds of that happening? What if she'd been with them? When she was in college, her dorm room had a gas leak and her roommate was found nearly dead. It had taken weeks for her to recover. Luckily for Avery, she'd fallen asleep in her study partner's room across the hall. Yeah. It was weird.

Even weirder were the feelings she brought out in me. I wanted to protect her, keep her safe. And it wasn't like I was desperate. I was a decent-looking guy, or so I'd been told. Although I managed to stay in shape for the job, I didn't spend nearly enough time at the gym. Ever since the divorce, I'd just been thinking about work, catching the bad guys, making the case, doing a decent job on the stand whenever I was summoned to court. I'd gotten into a rut. I was standing still.

Now it was time to move on. To try something new. Somewhere else.

All I could think about was Avery Dufresne, America's Newscaster. (*Note to self, never call her America's Sweetheart. She hates that with a passion.*)

Maybe it wasn't so strange to think that she and I could have something awesome together. Maybe the jock turned cop turned detective was good enough for a celeb turned philanthropist. My recent research didn't turn up much on the board she was on, but I knew she was loaded. Strange thing was, I didn't care if she was poor, broke or had bad credit. It sure hadn't mattered when I married Evelyn.

It didn't matter now either. I wanted to be with Avery, to be her protector, to be her rock. I was so serious that I had put in my application at the Mobile Police Department. I heard getting a detective position locally was super-competitive, but I was up to the task. I had a few things on my record that might make them pass me over, but if I could explain them, it would be okay. Those domestic violence allegations were bogus. I had never hurt Evelyn. Even when she slapped me or tried to run me over with her car. I simply left.

Well, we'd see soon. I had an interview on Monday. If this weekend went well, then I'd make sure I was there on time and I'd fight like hell to get the job. It was time to start over. I needed a "do-over" bad.

As if by magic, Avery called me. I answered with a laugh. "Hey! Were your ears burning?"

"Um, no. My ears are fine. Are yours? Are you sick?" I laughed at how she totally missed the joke. Perhaps I wasn't as funny as I thought.

"I mean to say, I've been thinking about you."

"Really? I have been thinking about you too. Are you in town yet?"

"No, I got a late start. Too much paperwork. Will you forgive me? I don't know if I'm going to make it in at a decent hour. Want to meet for breakfast? I can get a room at that bed and breakfast around the corner from you. What's it called again?"

"The Broken Egg. That would be fine. I'm kind of glad you aren't here yet. We had a long meeting, and I've got ghost hunters coming to Sugar Hill tonight. Something Miss Anne arranged." I could tell by the tone of her voice she wasn't thrilled. I didn't blame her. I wouldn't want a bunch of strangers tromping through my house either.

"That's wild! Will you be watching them? I think that might be kind of interesting to watch."

"Uh, no. I don't want to watch them. I think it's a bunch of bull. Sure, I believe in ghosts, but I don't think you can hunt them. And what are they going to do when they find them?" She sounded completely disgusted.

"Can't say no, huh?"

"Nope. It's what Anne wanted, but I don't have to make myself available for questions or film footage. I think I'm going home to pack a bag. I'll stay at Thorn Hill tonight. I'll be out of their way, and I can spend the night exploring the place. If you get in at a decent time, come surprise me. But call first. I'm packing now. I got my concealed-carry license, and I've been training every week."

"That's what I like to hear. Okay, well, if I do make it in at a decent hour, I'll call you. Don't shoot me, please, ma'am."

She laughed in the phone, and it was a pretty sound. She had a sexy voice. No wonder so many thousands of men liked listening to her every night. Or at least they did until she quit. "Don't you need the address? I don't think you've been here before."

Should I tell her my big secret now? Would she think I was some sort of weird stalker and refuse to speak to me again? "I can use my phone to find it, no worries. I'll see you either late tonight or in the morning."

"All right, well, call me when you get in if you aren't exhausted. I'll keep my phone by my bed."

"Okay. I'll do that. Night, until later."

"Night. Be safe, Jamie."

"You got it." I hung up the phone feeling like a million bucks.

Yeah, I was close to telling her my secret, but I didn't want to do it over the phone.

What would she say when she found out that I was a hometown boy? That I was from Belle Fontaine?

What would she say when she found out that my mother was a Dufresne who'd been rejected by the family she loved—cast off into foster care and forgotten? Of course, my mother never told me any of this. I had to dig it all up myself. She didn't have the courtesy to leave me a note before she drank herself to death.

What would Avery say when she found out that somehow, through a weird twist of fate, we were distant relatives?

I had a feeling she'd understand. I hoped so because I was head over heels for her already. And that I had not expected. It was an unusual feeling, an unusual attraction.

I had to keep her safe.

I didn't really understand what it meant, but the words were ringing in my head and in my heart. Now that I was driving eighty miles an hour and finally heading to Belle Fontaine, I could say them out loud.

Avery is my soul mate. She belongs to me. In another lifetime, she pledged herself to me. And now, I claim her. She is mine....

Chapter Three – Avery

I remembered the days when the sight of a television production truck thrilled me to pieces. This wasn't one of those days. Instead the sight of the ghost hunters' vans made my scar itch and my palms sweat.

"Come on, Avery! Get yourself together!" I coached myself as I eased closer to the house.

In the past three months I had refused umpteen interview requests, including repeated requests from my former producer, Amanda. What a lot of nerve she had asking me for anything! Especially after showing up here with Jonah—and the man who tried to kill me. Now the media was again invading my sanctuary, and the whole thing filled me with dread. I wanted the world to forget about me. What good had being America's Newscaster been? And what about News Quarter? Was I truly never going back? I had to admit it was looking that way.

I pulled my car into my spot and quickly got out. I hoped I might make it inside without being accosted by people from My Haunted Plantation, without them waving microphones in my face or "sweeping" me with electronic gadgets to verify I wasn't a ghost. I hoped in vain. The MHP team wasn't about to allow me to sneak inside without first greeting them. I could see that. One young woman walked toward me with a wave and a pleasant smile on her face. Despite my reservations, my protective shields dropped.

"Hi! You must be Avery Dufresne. Nice to meet you. I'm Jessica Chesterfield, and I'm with My Haunted Plantation. Thanks for letting us come and explore Sugar Hill." She stretched her hand toward me, and I shook it briefly. The reporter in me immediately began assessing her. Jessica was slightly shorter than me with a slender frame and a quiet voice. She wore a soft-looking blue shirt, light blue jeans and suede leather boots. She didn't look at all like a paranormal investigator. I didn't see any tattoos. I didn't mind them; I just thought girls who were into this sort of ghost hunting stuff might also be "goth." *Damn! I'm getting old—and far too judgmental.* No, she was the picture of an all-American girl and didn't look like someone who would spend her nights in a supposedly haunted house.

"Can I help you carry something?" she asked politely.

"No, I just have my purse. So you plan to investigate tonight?"

She nodded and immediately turned her attention to the house. Sugar Hill towered above us, and I looked up to follow her gaze. I didn't see anything out of the ordinary except that the windows in the Mirror Room appeared to be open. The curtains were hanging out and flapping in a nonexistent breeze. Jessica looked at me with a raised eyebrow, but I shrugged.

"My housekeeper is strange. She loves airing that room out. I think she's kind of obsessed with it. But then again, I guess you understand that. You must also be obsessed with old houses." I smiled at her, but she did not return my smile. And when she looked at me, she gazed past me, like she could see something near or around me, something I could not see. I shivered at the thought.

Okay, Avery. Keep it together, girl.

Jessica had long, wavy light brown hair that she wore down and naturally expressive blue eyes. If she wore a little makeup and dressed more professionally, she'd be a knockout. However, even as I thought it, I knew those sorts of things didn't matter to Jessica. She was exactly who she wanted to be. She liked herself and accepted others for who they were.

She'd always been that way, even when her brother lost her dog, Pet. She forgave him. Yes, she forgave him, but she'd secretly cried for two weeks. Then she went into the seventh grade and everything went wrong. She began to cut herself. Seemed like a stupid thing to do, but it helped her cope. Or so she thought. She didn't do that anymore, but she'd been tempted to when the pain became too great. Because it wasn't just about the dog. It was about the other thing. The thing she couldn't bear to think about. She had the scars to prove how much pain she'd been in...

I shook my head and told myself not to touch her hands again. It was too easy to connect with her. This weird linking, or whatever it was, had been happening too often recently. I hadn't been myself since I left the hospital.

"Are you okay, Miss Dufresne? You look like you've seen a ghost."

That brought me out of the trance I was in. I laughed at her turn of phrase. "No ghosts, not today."

"So what have you seen here? Your Aunt Anne said that..."

"No offense, Jessica, because you seem like a lovely person, but I don't want to be interviewed. Nor do I want to be involved in your ghost hunt in any kind of way. I am perfectly happy letting you guys do your thing, but if it had been left up to me, I would have said no. As it was Miss Anne's wish, I cannot refuse it."

"Oh, all right." Her eyes widened with surprise and she stammered, "Well, okay. But if you change your mind, we are perfectly happy interviewing you off camera. And we wouldn't have to use your name. In fact, we hadn't planned to mention you at all."

That was a surprise. I was the hottest thing in the newspaper today, or didn't she know that? But it did make me feel better. "Really? That seems hard to believe," I said suspiciously.

"I swear it's true. Here, I'll show you what we had in mind, Miss Dufresne."

"Please call me Avery."

With a nod she added, "Avery." She opened the back of the van, and I was shocked to see the incredible electronic setup inside. There were at least a dozen cameras, a computer that showed different readings, and shelves full of ominous-looking electronics. Somewhere in the background classic rock was playing.

"Here it is." She picked up a clipboard and handed it to me. I was careful to avoid touching her hands again. Everyone deserved their privacy, especially in their own head. Those were her private thoughts; I didn't want to intrude.

"Here's our hot sheet. It's kind of like an agenda we use on our investigations. We have two interviews scheduled, one with Robin Myron and another with Summer Dufresne. And that's it. You aren't on here at all. See? Your attorney, Reed, was very specific about that. We weren't to disturb you at all."

I didn't correct her—I knew what a hot sheet was, for Pete's sake. I scanned over it and flipped to the next page. This was a map of the house. "And the map? These are places you intend to investigate?"

She took it from me and tapped on the map. "Yes, we are going to check out the basement; Summer reports bad smells, whispers and strange feelings down there. We're also going up on the second floor to the Angel Gallery, and we'll be checking out the Mirror Room."

Merely hearing her mention the Mirror Room made my spine tingle. I didn't like that room at all, even though family history suggested it was one of Chase's favorite rooms. But then again, I knew Chase was not always a nice man.

"Well, good luck to you. I'm going to Thorn Hill. I'll be out of your way for the next what? Few days? How does that work for you?"

"That's more than long enough. We'll collect our data and then head to Thorn Hill for another two days. Then we head back home to examine it all. We'll have our report ready in a few weeks, but since Miss Anne is...no longer with us, maybe you would be willing to review our report? That was the one condition; she wanted to see the finished product before we aired it."

"Sure, Summer or I will review it. And when does the episode air?"

"Hmm...not sure about that. Maybe never. If we explore a house and it turns out to be a dud, then it never makes it to air. But..."

"But what?" I said as I hopped out of the van and waited for her to jump down.

"Well, I don't think that will be the case here. I can feel movement. You must have sensed their presence too. Have you seen anything here, Avery?"

"Why would you ask me that?"

"Just an intuition."

"Nice try, Jessica, but I don't have anything to share. Y'all be careful and stay out of my room, please. You are welcome to use any of the other rooms. Most are quite comfortable." With that I left her gawking after me on the porch. I guess she figured I would change my mind if she showed me her cards first, but there was too much to lose now. I wouldn't leave anything to chance if I didn't have to. She seemed like a nice person, but I had to stand firm.

So I'll be at Thorn Hill for a few days. I'd better go pack. At least I'll see Jamie!

It was dark out now, but as I bounded up the long staircase I could see someone was in my room. The door was open, and the bedside lamp was on.

What the hell? If this is one of the My Haunted Plantation people, they are going to wish they'd never walked in. I take my privacy seriously, as they're about to find out!

"Excuse me," I said angrily as I stepped in the doorway, expecting to call some pimply college student on the carpet. Right before my eyes, the bedside lamp flickered out. It looked like I was now alone in the room, but the fine blond hairs on my arms were raised up now like tiny alarm bells. What should I do? More than anything I wanted to escape the room, but I stood frozen to the spot. Then I heard the sound, the sound of a cabinet door banging repeatedly. Finding that my feet could actually move now, I walked around the bed and went to the bathroom door. I put my hand out to touch the doorknob when it began to twist, and then the door flew open.

I screamed my head off for five seconds. Summer, in a hair towel and a pink robe screamed back at me, "Holy crap, Avery! What the hell?"

I sat on the floor trying to breathe. "I'm sorry. I thought you were...an intruder."

"Dear God, calm down. I was just using your bathroom because someone was using mine. If I'd known I was going to a scream-fest, I would have waited and showered later. Good Lord, girl. What's up with you?" She leaned against the doorframe as she caught her breath.

I laughed with relief. So it wasn't a ghost in my room. Just my cousin in the shower, banging on the cabinet for whatever reason. The lamp obviously had a short in it. "What was with all the banging?"

"I wasn't banging. I thought someone was out here banging. That's why I got out of the shower. Was it you?"

"No, it wasn't me. It came from the bathroom."

She raised her hands and said, "Ha, ha—very funny. Now if you don't mind, I'm going to get dressed." She walked toward the door and tightened her robe. "I've got a date tonight—talk to you later." Summer sounded supremely aggravated, but that was her problem. She was so moody sometimes. Who was I kidding? I was the moody one lately.

"Fine. Me too. As a matter of fact, I am going to go stay at Thorn Hill for a couple of days. Jamie's on his way down."

Summer stopped and turned to me with a serious expression. "That's probably not the best idea. You haven't seen haunted until you visit there. Please, don't stay there. That place...it does things to people. Messes with their head. You know, I think that's one of the reasons why my brother is so *nuts*." She whispered the words like she was ashamed. Weren't all Dufresnes just a little nuts?

"Please stop. Don't tell me whatever you were going to tell me. I don't want to hear any family gossip about the place before I see it myself. I tell you what, though; I'll be willing to compare notes with you when I get back. Chances are I won't see anything."

"I hope you are right. That's a sad place; you can feel it when you walk in."

"How many times have you been there, Summer?"

She unwrapped her hair and ran her fingers through it. "Did you know that Miss Anne lived there for years? Rumor has it—I know you don't want to hear rumors, but you have to hear this one—rumor has it that Miss Anne kept a man there with her. Although she would not formally introduce him to us, we all saw him from time to time. Then one day, she collapsed in the house and Mitchell dragged her out and refused to let her go back. She fought him for a while, but she'd had a stroke and then cancer. She finally listened to reason. It's a sad place for sure."

"Who was the man?"

"Nobody knew, and Mitchell won't tell."

"Sounds like I'll have to ask him. Imagine, proper Miss Anne doing such a thing. I am dying to find out who he was."

"Good luck. I only saw him that once."

"You saw him?"

"Oh yeah, he was dressed up like one of those old-timey folks. With the suits...what do they call them? With the tails and collars?"

"Morning suits?"

"Yes, that's it. Well, I gotta go. My guy is taking me to Shell's Steak House."

"And who is *your* mystery man, Summer?"

"One of the guys from MHP. He's a cutie."

"What? Didn't you just meet him? Don't tell me you plan to hook up with one of the ghost chasers!"

"Stop being such a stick in the mud. Go on to Thorn Hill, but be careful. I'll hang out here, if you don't mind my using the Yellow Rose Room."

I walked along with her, feeling bad for acting like I was her judge. "That's fine. This is your home too, Summer. I like having you here."

"Good to hear that. See you when you get back. Enjoy yourself."

She pattered off down the hall, and I turned to walk back into my room. For the second time today I nearly screamed my head off. Jessica had snuck up behind me and was standing in front of me now.

Well, this is just about enough to make a nice girl want to cuss!

"You scared the hell out of me, Jessica!" I clutched my heart playfully and laughed. Jessica looked at me, but not quite. It was a weird thing. I watched her turn and walk into my room as if she were in a trance or something. I stared after her, but she didn't seem to notice. I walked back to the door feeling aggravated that she would invade my space when I plainly asked her not to.

That's it, I thought. *I'm about to end this crap now!*

Chapter Four – Avery

"Jessica, don't go in there, please." She ignored me and closed the door behind her. "Hey!" I was getting ticked. What a lot of nerve! I flung open the door and found no one in my room. As a matter of fact, I heard Jessica's voice behind me. She was talking to one of her team members.

"Okay, Becker, let's set it up at the end of this hall-way. Oh, hey! Are we in your way?"

"Um, no. You aren't, I mean, I think you aren't."

Becker smiled and waved as he went about his task and left Jessica and me alone in the hallway.

"Were you just in my room, Jessica?"

"No." She smiled curiously. "You just saw me come up those stairs. Why? What is it? Did you see some-one?"

"Yes, you! Do you have a twin on this team or some-one who looks a lot like you?"

"Definitely not. Why? I can see you are very upset. Are you all right? You're shaking. Avery, do you need to sit down?"

I leaned against the wall. Very upset did not begin to explain how I felt. "You aren't going to believe this, but I just saw you walk into my room. You looked right at me—it was totally you—but you didn't act like you could see me. You went in my room and shut the door."

"This door?"

"Yes," I said with a small nod.

She grabbed the walkie-talkie from her belt. "Hey, Beck, point that camera this way and come here. We've got some doppelganger action."

"Doppelganger? Did I hear you right?" Becker's voice crackled back over the walkie-talkie.

"Yep, come on. All right, Avery. Becker and I will sweep your room for anomalies. You want to come with us?"

"You aren't leaving me in the hallway."

Becker jogged toward us with a broad grin on his face. "Okay, let's finish the setup. I have a date tonight with a pretty lady." *Oh, so this is Summer's date. Hmm...* I reminded myself not to judge. He was at least nice to look at.

"Fine, but first things first. Let's sweep this room. Get some readings. It would be good to get a baseline before tonight."

"What time does your investigation begin?" I asked.

"Usually around midnight, sometimes later. We'll be here until about three. I promise we won't burn the house down."

I frowned. "Well, that's a relief."

I stood behind Jessica as she tapped on the door. What was she doing? Letting the ghost know we were coming in? I was pretty sure her ghost twin knew we were here.

"Excuse me," she said in her soft, pretty voice. "We don't mean to upset you, but we have to get in there. This is Avery's room now."

We didn't hear anything, so Jessica opened the door and immediately began walking around the room waving her electronic handheld device around. Becker recorded it all with his portable camera.

She sniffed the air. "Do you smell cigarettes in here? Are you a smoker, Avery?"

"I don't smell anything, and no, I don't smoke."

"I smell them too," Becker said.

"Maybe Summer was smoking; she used my shower. I'll ask her later."

"Look at this, Beck. The K2 unit is surging here in this corner."

He grunted and said, "Switching to thermal."

"So, if you are here, and you can hear me, I want you to know we aren't here to harm you. We just want to talk to you. I am going to set this meter down right here. If you touch it, it will light up. See?" She put the electronic device on my bed and waved her hand across the front of it, causing it to beep. Jessica continued talking to the empty room, "Like that. I won't hurt you. Can you try it?"

"Are we supposed to talk to it?" It must have heard me because the machine began beeping like crazy.

Jessica ignored me and said, "Let's use the EVP. I'll ask some questions." I didn't wait any longer. I grabbed my tote bag from the closet and began stuffing clothes and my cosmetics into it. I wasn't sticking around for this nonsense. "Wait, Avery. It's perfectly safe. Let me explain how it works."

"No, I'm sorry. I can't do this, Jessica. Sorry." I walked out the door without another word. I was down the stairs and in the car before you could say boo. As I backed the car up to make a break for it at long last, I heard a tap on my window. It was Handsome Cheever. I rolled the window down and tried to calm my breathing.

Handsome's eyes were large and white, and I could tell he was upset. Handsome took spiritual matters seriously, and rightly so. He knew having the television show here was bad news.

"I know, I know, Handsome. I think this is a bad idea too, but it was Miss Anne's wish. There's nothing I can do about it."

"Oh, it's not that, Miss Dufresne. It's not that at all. No, you see, Miss Billie's been singing. She's singing a sad tune now. Something bad is gonna happen. I don't want nothing bad to happen to you. You've got to leave this place and let me purify it with salt. That will help keep these old spirits away. I can see them gathering. She sees them gathering—and she's singing up a storm. Oh please, Miss Dufresne, let me help you."

"Handsome, I am fine, but I have to go away for a few days. When I get back, all these people will be gone and we'll go back to having our privacy. And then you can pour as much salt as you like. But now I have to go! I'd like to get to Thorn Hill before it gets any later."

"Oh no, Miss Dufresne! Anywhere but there! That's where he wants you to be. That's where he is! He's going to claim you, just like he tried to claim Miss Anne and the one before her. Please don't go there. He's evil!"

I could hardly follow what he was talking about, and he was beginning to frighten me worse than the lamp, the banging and the ghost doppelganger. "Now really, I have to go, Handsome. I will be okay. My friend Jamie is coming to see me, and he has a gun. So do I!" I smiled at him with a confidence I did not feel.

He stepped back with tears in his eyes. "It won't matter, Miss. Haven't you ever heard of 'familiar spirits'?

That's what the man is—the man in black. And it won't matter if you have a gun at all because he's already dead. And Miss Billie is singing up a storm for you. She says to tell you that if you lie with that familiar spirit, you will never be able to get rid of him. He'll have you forever! Don't do it! You won't do it, will you?"

"Handsome! Of course I won't. Don't say such things! This isn't an appropriate topic of conversation," I tried to reason with him, but I could see I wasn't getting through. "Now, please. I have to go. Go home and get some rest. I'll be back in a few days."

I pulled out of the driveway and couldn't help but look in the rearview mirror. I didn't see Billie Holiday, just Handsome standing there in his black suit and white shirt with his chauffeur's hat perched neatly on his head. He waved at me sadly and slowly.

Like he thought he'd never see me again.

PART TWO

Chapter Five – Summer Dufresne

I didn't care what bull crap Reed was telling Avery. If it had been me, I never would have let those nosy bastards inside Sugar Hill. Of course we had ghosts, but they were *our* ghosts. And they had secrets. *We* had secrets—secrets that should be kept to ourselves. What would happen if the viewing public discovered those secrets? The truth was dangerous, and I didn't even dare think about it. At least I was *trying* to keep an eye on things.

This Becker guy would tell me everything I wanted to know—if there was anything to know. I was looking forward to digging it out of him.

With a bored sigh, I focused on drying my hair, which was always a chore because it was so long now. Recently I toyed with the idea of cutting it, but why start now? I mean, I did get the occasional trim, just to keep it healthy and keep it from being freakishly long. I loved my hair; it was my best feature. I quickly finished my makeup and put on a light blue dress that fit me perfectly. I slid on my cowboy boots and then reached inside my purse for my perfume. This was a new scent, and I was eager to give it a try. Smiling at the mirror, I checked my mouth for toothpaste and gave myself an approving nod. Yep, I was date-ready.

I walked out of the room and found Becker texting on the stairs. The lights were still on, thankfully, but the show's written request said they would like to keep them off. And Becker didn't say so exactly, but I could tell they preferred the house to be empty of living inhabitants.

I didn't like the idea of being in the house in complete darkness while they held their investigation. What I'd told Avery wasn't completely true. No way was I staying the night. I'd be back here in the morning, just to keep an eye on things and do the interview, but I was going to book a room at the Broken Egg Bed and Breakfast. That would be more comfortable. Not to mention private. It wasn't a fancy hotel, but it would serve its purpose. Before I could greet him with a sexy kiss as I planned, my phone rang. I thought about not answering, but I recognized the number.

Nope. Couldn't avoid this one.

"Yes, this is Summer."

"Good evening. I hope I didn't catch you too late. Probably getting ready for bed?"

"Not too late. What's up, Pepper?" It was best to give my cousin as little information as possible. She was one to be nosey. That was for sure. I walked by Becker and smiled at him flirtatiously, and he followed me down the stairs like an obedient dog. I waved my keys at him and tossed them in his direction. I couldn't avoid this phone call, but I was doing my best to keep it short. "How can I help you?"

"So very kind of you to ask, but you always were that kind of young lady. So kind and caring." I rolled my eyes at her words but didn't say anything. "Anyway, I guess you heard about the meeting, about your brother being nominated and named the newest board member."

"What are you talking about?"

"The matrone named him the new board member."

Oh, I see what's going on, Pepper. Avery put a bee in your bonnet, and now you want me to kill it. Well, I can't help you. Miss Anne cut me off, and it's not my problem anymore.

But I thought about it and remembered it was best to play peacemaker, at least until I could gather the facts.

"Mitchell will make a nice addition to the board. Thank you for voting for him. You did, didn't you?"

"Well, yes. I signed the book. He's the new board member, but I have to tell you—because I know I can be honest with you, Summer. Avery didn't do things the right way. She should have stayed out of it and let the system work, just like we've always done. It upsets things when they aren't done the right way. She should not be allowed to step in and change everything. I swear, if Aunt Anne had seen her jump in the middle of that meeting, she would be turning in her grave. And to think she bumped you out of the way and put Avery in there. That's just wrong. I never agreed with her on that. It was not right. Not at all, dear."

My hair stood up at her last statement. What did Pepper know about my private business? Why was she telling me this? I was sure she wanted to rile me up and get me going so I'd agree to become her ally. I didn't work that way. I was a long-term planner, not an officious old lady with a personal agenda.

"Pepper, I can tell that you are very upset, but this isn't the way to resolve the issue. If I were you, I would call Avery and get this off your chest. Tell her how you feel; explain to her how things work. She'll understand, and she'll be glad that you are helping her."

"She is a strong-minded young woman. I don't think she'd welcome my advice. But maybe you could talk to her and tell her everything she needs to know."

"I'm not going to do that—and neither are you. You all will have to work it out."

After a long pause, Pepper said in a voice not much above a whisper, "What does she know? Does she have any clue about...anything?"

"I'm sure she knows what she needs to. You should be asking Reed about that. Not me."

"I see," she said, obviously disappointed.

Why was she giving me a hard time? As if I could do anything about Avery's predicament. I added, "And may I remind you—she wears the ring now. You can't change that, Pepper. Anne did that. I think it's out of everyone's hands at this point. Now I have to go. Good night." I pushed the red "End Call" button and slid the phone in my clutch purse.

"That sounded intense," Becker said with a grin. He had looks in spades, but I got the feeling he wasn't too smart. Oh well, that didn't matter. I didn't need him to build me a house, just fiddle with a few of the knobs. And tell me what he knew, if anything. I smiled innocently and chitchatted with him about what it was like working on a television series. I didn't really care. Until this unexpected intrusion, I had never heard of the show.

The whole time he talked, which was a long time, I nodded and smiled. He littered his narrative with complete descriptions on how to set up multiple cameras on one source, and a bunch of other useless information I had no wish to remember. Again, I nodded and smiled as if I, a simple country girl, were greatly entertained and impressed with his vast "Hollywood" knowledge.

This was what my mother called ego-stroking. It was something a Southern girl had to learn, she would say. It was part of her training. I let him brag about his ghost hunts while I thought about my conversation with Pepper. No, I couldn't let this go. I had to call my cousin. He needed to know that there was dissension in the ranks. How to end this monologue and make my call?

"Shoot. Looks like we need some gas, Becker. Let's stop here. Won't take a second."

"Really? Cause it looks okay to me."

"I know, but the gauge is broken. Let's top it off, just to be sure. I'd hate to get stranded on the side of the road. It takes forever to get a tow out here. I think maybe ten should do it."

I began to dig in my purse when he interrupted me, "No, I've got this."

"Oh...thanks." *Wow. Big spender.* I dialed Reed's number and watched Becker walk inside the Quick Mart. I was beginning to have second thoughts about my plans. Did I really need to go all the way with this guy? I could get all the info I needed if I were just willing to listen to him talk long enough.

"Hey, Reed, it's me. Yeah, just left the house. Going to show one of the crew members around. He's got some time to kill before the investigation gets started."

"Is that a good idea? Never mind. Don't answer that—just be careful," he said.

"Always. Listen, Pepper called me just a minute ago. She was complaining about Mitchell's board appointment. Why didn't you tell me?"

"I figured your brother would. He didn't?"

"No. He practically lives at the Rose Cottage now. I never see him, but I guess you knew that."

"It's his home. I don't begrudge him that little shack. Miss Anne wanted him there."

"Miss Anne!" I mocked. "I am so tired of hearing about her." I flopped back against the seat and said, "Listen, Pepper is going to stir stuff up with the rest of the board. I can just about guarantee that. She's got a bug in her hat, and she's not ready to let it go. I don't know what you can do, but you'll have to deal with it. I can't. And she's threatening to talk to Avery. Tell her about you-know-who."

"Okay, and?" He sounded bored. Why did I even bother?

"And...well, she kind of suggested that I should be matrone."

"And what did you say to that?"

I blew my bangs out of my eyes. "I reminded her that Avery had the ring. And I didn't say, 'Hey, let's cut it off of her finger.'"

"Thanks for telling me about this. I'll keep my eyes peeled and handle her."

"Well, don't hurt her. She's just an old lady with too much time on her hands."

He didn't make any promises but asked in a low voice, "What do you think? If something happened to Avery, would you be willing to step into her shoes?"

"What? That's...you must be joking. I don't want to be matrone. You and I both know the cost. Would you really wish that on me, Reed?"

"Who says it has to be that way? I never put much stock in curses and such. And it's just a ring."

"A ring and a ghost," I reminded him sarcastically.

"If you say so. Don't stay out too late."

He hung up without another word. I turned my phone on silent and slid it into my purse.

Becker climbed back in the car and put on his seat belt. I reached over and touched his cheek. "You know what? I'm not very hungry right now. Let's go get that room. I mean, I'm going to need somewhere to stay tonight, right? And they do have room service, or at least some vending machines."

Becker grinned and agreed. In a few minutes, we were in the driveway of the Broken Egg. I slipped out of the vinyl seat and walked inside to book the room.

I knew he was watching me walk, so I swished my hips playfully as I made my way across the broken driveway. I looked back and could see him grinning. Poor guy, I hoped he was okay with just hooking up once. I rarely saw a guy more than that. It just wasn't my thing.

I was never going to get married. Never! If I might ever become matrone, it was better to not love than to love and watch my husband die. At the hands of a jealous ghost.

Just ask Vertie and Anne.

That's what happened to all the Dufresne husbands; at least those whose wives served as matrones and had been touched by the Lovely Man.

And I had seen him. And he had seen me. And once wanted me. But that was before....

I told only one person about that day. Vertie.

I had lied to Avery when I said I never met her. I did know her, but if I had told Avery I would have had to explain about the ghost. Vertie knew—she knew I saw the "Lovely Man," as Cousin Maggie used to call him. Yes, Vertie knew this, and she knew that he kissed me. Apparently she had not shared our secret with Avery. Someone should have, but it wasn't my decision to make. That had been the board's call, and Reed's and Miss Anne's. And even Vertie's. But Avery was smart; she probably would find out about it without my help. He was probably reaching for her now—seducing her! Yes, she could find a way to resist him.

Someone would tell her. *Maybe I would.* I wasn't sure yet, for I hadn't truly made up my mind that I liked her that much.

And if she was dead, I would be matrone. Once, I would have cut off her finger to claim the ring, but not now.

I pulled Becker to me and kissed him passionately. He followed me to our room. Once we got inside, I drowned myself in his cheap drugstore cologne and smooth skin. It was a pleasant experience, but at the end of it I felt empty. I was still searching for the satisfaction I so desired. Becker stroked my hair and wanted pillow talk, but I wanted to sleep. And I did.

I dreamed about *him* again. I knew his name. I'd learned that on my own.

Ambrose...

The Lovely Man...

He had white teeth. They were slightly too large, but he had a sexy smile. His eyes were dark but not empty—they were hungry. Hungry for me. He had a feather in his hand—no, it was a leaf. He was rubbing it across my forehead while he whispered in my ear. He spoke my name, but he wanted me to never say his. Somehow I knew that. And I was too afraid to disobey him. I had been warned all my life not to. Although I never said it, I thought his name often. At least in my dreams. Ambrose's dark hair fluttered about him as if it were catching a breeze that blew in from his dark spirit world. He had an earthy, spicy smell; it was a strange perfume that intoxicated me and numbed me to the consequences of being with him, at least for a little while. I remembered reading Anne's diary one day and seeing the scent described as "the smell of enchantment." That was as good as any description I could come up with.

And then he vanished and left me writhing with desire on my bed.

But it didn't matter anymore, did it? He would choose the one who had the ring, and that filled me with sorrow. He must—he was bound to it just as he had been from the beginning. Even though I knew all that, God help me, it didn't matter.

I wanted Ambrose. And I would do anything to have him claim me.

Even if that meant stealing the ring. However I could.

Chapter Six – Avery

Everyone told me how much Thorn Hill looked like Sugar Hill, but I'd had no idea how right they were. Thorn Hill was not as grand, as it was built on a smaller scale, but not by much. And like the name suggested, it was an unwelcoming place, a place of shadows.

How strange was it that both of these two old houses were in such good shape? And the familial continuity was also very unusual. Most of the time old houses such as Sugar Hill passed to different families. That wasn't the case with these properties. How had the Dufresnes managed that? And another question that burned in the back of my mind—how had they managed to procure so much wealth and yet largely stay under the radar of the local community?

Why was I thinking about this?

Because I am sitting in the driveway of a spooky-looking house where I'm spending the next two nights.

Perhaps I should have stayed at Sugar Hill instead of freaking out about My Haunted Plantation. Well, I was here now. Might as well make the best of it. At least the front porch light was on.

Unlike at Sugar Hill, there wasn't much open space at the front of the house. Two large pecan trees leaned toward Thorn Hill, like skeletal arms reaching for the home. There were also several other trees on

the property, including a magnolia that had somehow managed to hold on to a few of its waxy green
leaves. Grass did not stand a chance at growing here;
there was far too much shade for a luxurious lawn.
Taking my foot off the brake, I let the car roll across
the driveway and held my breath as I passed under
the tree branches. It was as if they were some sort of
arboreal gateway—one that would lead me to the
past. Perhaps my car would transform into an old-
fashioned carriage. No such luck. My Lexus was still a
car and the house, still beautiful and forlorn-looking,
awaited me.

Man, I must be more exhausted than I thought.

Clouds above me parted, and the moon shined down
upon me for a few seconds before more dark clouds
skittered in front of it. It was early to be this dark,
but that was how it was this time of year—early eve-
nings, early mornings. I grabbed my tote bag and
headed for the front door. All I had to do was walk
up the steps and unlock the place. I owned it, right?
So what was my problem? Why was I lingering on
the porch like a shy girl selling Girl Scout cookies?

Because I feel like an intruder, that's why!

I poked out my chin and stomped up the steps. I had
the keys in my hand, and I noticed they were shaking. Not my hand but the keys. Surprised, I dropped
them on the wooden porch. As I reached down to
pick them up, I heard a noise not far from me. It
sounded like heavy footfalls. A man's footfalls. Yes,

someone was running around the wraparound porch, trying to keep me from seeing them. A fall breeze sent pecans down on me. The hard hulls pelted my car, and a few branches slapped the roof of the porch. The freshly painted white porch swing moved, seemingly on its own volition, but I realized that too was likely just the wind.

"Hello?" I called to the side of the house where I'd heard someone running. No one answered. Whoever had run from me was gone now. Best to get inside and sort things out.

The keys weren't shaking now—surely that had been my hand. I managed to get the key into the door. It clicked easily and opened without a sound.

The front room was full of shadows, and my hands immediately began searching for a light switch. I found one, but the dim lights that the switch commanded did not do much to brighten up the room. No, this was not a cheerful place at all. There was no portrait of Chase Dufresne here. In the place where the painting of Chase hung at Sugar Hill was the painting of a black dog with a bright red collar. Still, there was enough light to see the odd scene. Yes, indeed, this place did look very much like Sugar Hill. I had the eerie sense that Thorn Hill was a life-size dollhouse. And that if I looked hard enough I would find that the appliances didn't work, that the furniture was plastic and that everything here was an illusion.

"Hello? Is there anyone here? It's me, Avery Dufresne." I closed the door behind me as I hauled my tote bag inside. "Hello?" I waited another minute but heard nothing at all. Reed said that there was a housekeeper here, but besides the footsteps I had not seen or heard anyone. *Hmm...should I call him?* I thought better of that, especially after our conversation earlier. No, better to call Summer to see what was up. I didn't want to surprise anyone by showing up unannounced.

"Hey, Summer? Sorry to bother you, but I'm at Thorn Hill and there is no one here."

"Oh yeah, the housekeeper there goes home at night. There is no overnight staff at Thorn Hill. Sorry, I reckon I should have told you that. Check the refrigerator, though. I am sure she loaded it up for you, and the master bedroom should be all ready. Do you want me to ask Robin to go up there? I don't really need her at Sugar Hill tonight."

"Oh no. I don't need anyone to wait on me. I am sure it will be fine. Just wanted to check. You know, I thought I heard someone here, but it must have been the wind."

"Probably so. Anything else?" I could tell Summer was busy, and I thought it might be fun to tease her.

"How is the date going?"

"Well, I could tell you, but then I'd have to kill you."

When I didn't laugh, she did. "God, Avery. You have got to learn how to take a joke. You've been in the city too long, cousin. I'll talk to you in the morning. Bye!"

And that was it. So unless Jamie showed up, which was looking more doubtful, it was just me here. I took a deep breath, grabbed my bag and started to take it upstairs when I stopped. I felt eyes staring at me. I slowly surveyed the room and whispered once more, "Hello?"

Then I spotted her: a beautiful woman staring down at me from above the parlor fireplace! It was a massive painting, taking up much of the space above the mantelpiece. The colors were vivid and bright, even in the half light. Turning on a lamp, I walked into the room to take in the full picture. My! She was lovely, and I knew right away who she was. She was none other than Susanna Serene Dufresne. Even if I had been too dense to identify her, her name had been lovingly etched on a gold panel at the bottom of the portrait. She was the woman I'd seen in the woods, the one at the well, the one who'd haunted the house in search of her baby. Had she found peace? I shivered and imagined I heard a voice whisper, *No*.... The wind was whistling around the eaves of the house now, and I could hear the porch swing squeaking.

The harder I stared, the weirder the picture seemed to me. Susanna was standing outside Sugar Hill, or was that Thorn Hill? It was as if she were ready to lead a lost party into the safety of the house. She held a golden candelabra in both hands, and the light reflected off her shiny lavender gown and illuminated her beautiful face. So much detail! Yes, the harder I looked, the more I saw. I could see the dark eyelashes that encircled her eyes, the mouth poised to speak a word or blow a kiss. I could clearly see her dark purple eyes, her dark brown hair and the sheer perfection of her facial features. She was the picture of loveliness—even her hands were lovely. No wonder Chase loved her when he first saw her, and no wonder Ambrose wanted to possess her. I shivered at the thought.

"Aren't you beautiful, Susanna? Thank you for lighting a candle for me," I said with honest appreciation. I noticed a few other strange details in the painting. In the greenery of the trees I thought I spotted a pair of eyes, and at the hem of her skirt there was a broken glass.

Unless my eyes were deceiving me—and they must have been—one of the lights of her candelabra flickered. I gasped in surprise and stepped closer, ignoring the increasing cold in the room. I stared even harder, but it didn't happen again. I walked out of the room, refusing to look back in case I saw Susanna missing from the frame entirely and standing in the room in front of me. I didn't feel that she'd hurt me, but things were very strange here.

You could sense it in the air.

It wasn't empty; it was thick with the presence of something—no, someone.

Yes, very strange indeed. Maybe I should turn around. Then I would see there was no one there. All was as it should be here in this strange house.

Before I could muster the courage to challenge whatever lurked here, the phone in the front room rang. Like a scared rabbit, I flew to the phone and snatched it up like it was my last chance to talk to a living person.

Maybe it was.

Chapter Seven – Avery

I fumbled with the receiver as I picked it up. "Yes? Yes? May I help you?"

"Avery? Are you all right? You sound out of sorts."

"Yes, I'm fine." My hands were shaking, and so was my voice.

"This is Reed."

"I knew that. Hi, Reed."

"Just making sure you got settled in. Everything okay at Thorn Hill? Would you like me to bring you something for dinner?"

"Oh," I said with a smile, "that's so thoughtful, but I haven't even thought of supper. Gee, what time is it?"

He laughed softly. "It's well past dinnertime. Are you sure you're okay?"

"Yes, it's just this house. I thought I heard someone running down the porch when I got here, but I must have imagined it." *And some other things.*

"I gave you fair warning about Thorn Hill. It has a definite 'gothic' vibe. Have you changed your mind, Avery? Do you want me to check around for a room?"

"No way. It's just that I thought someone was here. I have no doubt all will be well. I don't need any rescuing, Reed. This is the modern era, you know."

"I don't mean to come off as old-fashioned. I know you are no wilting flower. Thanks for being a good sport about all this. I wonder what the old girl was thinking when she wrote those ghost hunters. It's really out of character for her. She did not like television much, so I doubt she watched a single episode of My Haunted Plantation. But there's nothing we can do about it."

I got the distinct impression that Reed wasn't being entirely sincere, but my nerves were too frayed to question him further. "Yes, you gave me fair warning. Well, I have to go. I haven't even made it upstairs yet."

I heard another sound, coming from upstairs. It sounded like...laughter. A man's laughter, deep but not humorous at all. And it was not of this world. I had heard it before—at Sugar Hill. *Okay, how is that possible? Am I totally nutso now? Who ever heard of a ghost haunting two locations?* My skin tingled, and I felt cold suddenly. "You know what, Reed? I *would* like something to eat. I am sure I can find some coffee or tea in the kitchen."

"Terrific! I'll be there soon. Give me fifteen minutes."

"Wonderful. See you soon."

I left my bag at the bottom of the stairs, refusing to make the trip upstairs alone, and walked into the kitchen. Since the place was arranged like Sugar Hill, I took a guess at where to find everything. I put on a pot of coffee; I wouldn't normally do that at this hour, but it seemed like a normal thing to do. I needed normal. I flipped on every light I could and even found a stereo in the dining room. I pushed play on the CD player; I couldn't care less who the artist was. I just wanted some music to fill the air. I didn't want to hear any more laughter or whispers or anything else. I breathed a sigh of relief. The music that poured out of the shiny black speakers was a lovely instrumental from some half-forgotten romance movie. It was moody but light, and I hummed along as I searched the cabinets for plates, forks, napkins and of course some good old normal coffee.

I set the small breakfast table. No sense in eating in the big dining room if it was just the two of us. About the time I got everything settled and found a pretty candle to light, the doorbell rang. I was happy to see Reed's face through the slit of glass in the big cedar door.

"Hey!" I said as I opened the door. "Come on in."

"I hope you were in the mood for something simple. I grabbed us a muffuletta and some fries."

"Perfect. Let's eat in the kitchen."

"Sure," he said with a warm smile. He'd shed his fitted suit and dress shoes for a pair of blue jeans and a red polo shirt. He looked as if he'd just stepped out of the shower—his dark hair was still wet, and he smelled like a million bucks. Awful nice of him to dress up for me when he didn't have to.

"Sorry," I said, "I haven't had a chance to change yet. It's been crazy the past few hours. Those ghost hunters had things stirred up before I even left. I was ready to get out of there. Have you met that Jessica girl?"

"What do you mean stirred up?" He paused his unpacking the bag of food.

"I mean stirred up." I didn't really want to talk about it. Not yet.

He didn't push the issue. "You got any ketchup?"

"Search me. I didn't look around the kitchen much. I'm lucky I found the coffee."

He got up to find the ketchup and grabbed a few other things too. Apparently the house staff had left the kitchen pantry well stocked. That was good to know. By the time we finished our food, I was stuffed and in definite need of changing my clothes. How had I managed to get ketchup on my shirt? We laughed at the mess we made.

"Wait! You can't quit before dessert. I have beignets." I had to admit having a few beignets to snack on would be the perfect way to end the meal. I'd already made a pig of myself. I dug through the bags, convinced he was hiding them from me. "Where did you put them?"

He tied on an apron and began pouring a box of ingredients into a bowl. "This is the best kind. You make them, you don't buy them."

"No, I can't ask you to cook for me." I frowned at him. This seemed wrong all of a sudden. Was he just being polite, or did he think this was some kind of date? Growing up with no family, no cousins, I wasn't sure what the protocol was here. I opened my mouth to ask, unsure how I'd form the sentences without hurting him, but the doorbell interrupted me. I left him to heat up the grease and roll out the dough. Sweet mood music continued in the dining room. I decided to shut it off.

I walked to the front door and sure enough, it was Jamie Richards. He waved at me, and I couldn't resist hugging him as soon as I opened the door. "I am so happy to see you, detective!"

"None of that 'detective' nonsense," he said with a small smile. "Tonight I'm just Jamie. Hey, what smells so good?"

I gave him a sheepish look and whispered, "Reed's here. He's making beignets."

"Ooh...perfect timing, then. I'm starving." We stood awkwardly for a moment. It seemed like he wasn't sure whether to hug me or kiss me, so I decided to take the lead. I kissed him and took his hand, leading him into the delicious-smelling kitchen. The men greeted one another like they were best friends even though they'd only met a couple of times.

"How's it going, detective? Atlanta PD been keeping you busy?"

"You know it, but I'm hoping that will change soon."

"How's that?" Reed asked as he nudged a beignet around the pan.

"You want some coffee?" I asked Jamie.

"Sounds great. I'll take it black, please." He turned back to Reed and said, "I'm thinking of taking some time off soon. I've had some other opportunities come up. Might mean moving closer to you all."

"Really? You ought to think about Mobile. They've got a top-notch department with a new police chief. I hear he's looking for a few good detectives. Might be worth looking into."

"Thanks." Jamie accepted the mug of hot coffee and blew across the top of it before taking a sip. "Funny you should say that." He smiled at me and continued, "I guess I should have mentioned this to you before, but I've applied for a position here in Mobile County. I won't know anything until later this week. But I'd like to get out of the city, and I've kind of fallen in love with the area here." His handsome face reddened.

"Good for you," I said. I didn't want to rush our relationship, and I hoped he didn't either, but I liked the idea of him being closer. Reed seemed happy about it, to his credit, and promised to check in on the matter.

"Don't go to any trouble, Reed. I'm happy to see how it plays out."

"It's no trouble, but if you don't want me to mention it to Chief Harper, I won't."

"Thanks." Jamie looked at me. "Are you okay? You seem kind of quiet."

"Oh, it's been a day. But yeah, I'm great."

The two guys shot the breeze a little longer while Reed finished frying the beignets. When he was done, he tossed them in confectioners' sugar and put the plate in front of us.

"Here you go, folks." He removed his apron and tossed it on the counter. I wondered if he intended for me to clean this mess up. "The housekeeper will take care of this, Avery. So don't worry over it. I've got to go—I had no idea it had gotten so late."

"We would love to visit with you some more. You sure you can't stay?" I asked hopefully. Everything seemed normal with Reed here.

"You know what the French say, 'Three is a crowd.'"

I shook my head and chuckled. "I'd guess that is exactly the *opposite* of what the French say, but point taken. Nobody likes to be the third wheel, although you aren't. At least let me return the favor. Come have some breakfast with me in the morning. Say about nine?"

"You twisted my arm." He kissed my cheek and patted Jamie on the back. "Got to go. See you then." We followed him to the front door. Before he turned to leave, he looked at Jamie and said, "Take care of her."

Jamie's light brown eyes widened as he nodded.

"Excuse me, you two," I said, "I'll have you know I have a gun. And I'm not afraid to use it."

"Good. In that case, you take care of him. Good night to you both."

I shut the door and locked it. Jamie was rubbing my shoulders, and I didn't pull away.

"You know, I was just thinking how I would like to kiss your neck. I don't think I've done that yet."

I turned around and slid my arms around his neck. "Were you?"

"Yes, I was. Would you mind?" In a whisper he said, "All I could think about on the way here was you, kissing you, holding you...being with you. What about you? Have you thought about me, Avery?"

"Well... I..." Before I could give him my answer, something upstairs crashed so loudly that it reverberated through my body.

"What the hell was that? Sounded like a chandelier or something! Anyone else here?"

"Not that I know of."

"Stay here while I go up."

"Not on your life, buddy." I dug in my purse and grabbed my gun. He slid his out from his shoulder holster. We ran up the stairs, my heart beating fast, my hands as sweaty as they could be. I hoped I didn't drop the gun. At least the safety was on. "Hey! If you're up here, show yourself! You've got to the count of three!" Jamie called in his cop voice. His big arms tensed as he leaned against the wall and swung out to face whoever was in the hall. He had waved me back, so I stayed in place.

"Who are you? I can see you!"

Jamie's voice sounded different; was that fear I heard?

"Who is it, Jamie?" He didn't answer right away, and before he could, a loud pop took out the lights. The two of us stood in the dark on the second floor.

I whispered, "There are lanterns in the kitchen. I saw them in the pantry."

"Okay, so let's take it nice and slow. Step back slowly. Careful going down the stairs."

"You saw someone didn't you, Jamie?"

"Avery, do as I say. Walk down the stairs. I'm right with you, okay?"

"Okay." I felt my skin crawling as I walked down the stairs slowly. It was totally black in here. If I could get to my cell phone in the kitchen, we'd be okay. With that thought, I turned to feel my way into the kitchen.

And I did indeed feel something. Or someone.

Chapter Eight – Jessica Chesterfield

"I can't believe this. We've been here for hours with nothing to show for it. Not even a flicker on a REM pod." Megan cracked her gum, a clear indication that she was ticked off at the ghosts of Sugar Hill. "Is this a joke?"

"Are the REM pods on? Is this a battery drain?" Becker sounded hopeful. If that were true, it would at least mean we had some activity, even if it was negative activity. Battery drains often accompanied the manifestation of negative entities. At least that's what we'd experienced. They seemed to draw energy from power sources like batteries and electromagnetic fields.

"Can't be battery drain," Megan said, chewing her gum even faster. "They are working fine. Look on the monitors. I've got six cameras up, and there's nothing. Not even the odd shadow creature. Not battery loss. So far, we've got nothing. I thought this was the hottest spot in the county, Mike."

Mike was the boss, or at least the field boss. He didn't say much but stared at the cameras intently. He was a true believer, but he liked to pretend he was a skeptic. That was the only way he could successfully pitch the show. The people at the Paranormal Channel had enough programming featuring the proponents of the paranormal. They wanted to present opposing viewpoints, and that was where My

Haunted Plantation came into play. We were supposed to be disproving these hauntings.

"What do you think, Jess?" Mike glanced up at me.

I crossed my arms and chewed on my lip as I stared at the camera feeds. "Oh, the ghosts are here, all right. They're just hiding from us." I stared at Camera Three. It was in the basement, my least favorite location in the rambling old house. My brother used to say, "This place has bad vibes." And Sugar Hill did. Something sinister lingered there and wanted to remain undetected. It liked being alone. I felt my spine tingle, as if someone had poured ice water down my back.

Megan stopped chewing her gum and reached for a walkie-talkie. "Well, let's shake things up, chickie. I'm going in. You coming?" She slid the radio on her hip and straightened her black MHP hat. Megan was taller than me and had way more curves. She didn't have a problem hamming up our hunts for the camera while I preferred to hang out in the background. I liked the way we worked together. She treated me with respect, at least on camera. She listened to what I had to say, but she was one to make up her own mind about things. That's how she rolled, as she told me time and time again.

"Yep." Mike handed me a digital recorder and said, "Why don't you guys start in the basement?" My eyes widened at the prospect as I nodded. Mike never talked much about his superpowers of ghost detection, but I suspected he had them. "And don't forget to wait a few seconds between questions, Megan."

"Then let Jessica ask the questions this time." She rolled her eyes and tossed her gum in the small garbage can. Once upon a time, Megan and Mike had a thing, but the red-hot flames of that relationship had died out over the summer. We typically took summers off and did our hunts in fall and winter. When we all got back together again this past fall, the two barely spoke to one another. It had been awkward for a while, but now it was just something we didn't talk about. Besides, the show execs didn't encourage that sort of thing. The focus of the show wasn't to discuss our personal lives—much less have one outside the show.

No worries for me. I hadn't had a date in over a year, and it had been much longer than that since my last intimate encounter. Sometimes that bothered me, but most times I didn't think much about it. I spent my time reading books, studying up on hauntings that interested me and keeping up with my blog. If there was ever a nerd girl, it was me.

We jumped out of the back of the van and walked up the sidewalk that led to the house. It was windy tonight, and I was glad I wore my fleece-lined jacket, a gift from my parents last Christmas. I zipped it up and shoved my hands in the pockets. "Watch your step here," I warned the cameraman who followed us into Sugar Hill. Someone had left a bunch of cables in the walkway, which made for a major tripping hazard. It would be difficult to see them while peering through a camera lens.

"Thanks," he muttered. His name was James, if I remembered correctly—he was new and quite the nervous type. Not the kind of guy you would think would be part of a ghost hunting group.

As Megan opened the door and we stepped inside the house, a hush fell over the place. A spiritual hush. As a sensitive, I was responsible for "feeling" what was around us. There was usually something, residual evidence of some trauma or tragedy, but this place was remarkably clear at the moment. It hadn't been that way earlier. I'd definitely detected a strong female presence and a male presence lingering around the edges. Yes, this place practically sighed under the weight of its secrets.

As always, the lights were out. That was how we conducted all MHP investigations. It made the film look spookier, but other than that I honestly didn't see any advantage to stumbling around in the dark. I didn't think the ghosts cared either, except for the kind you didn't want to meet. I felt a weird sensation in my side, as if I'd been running and had a catch in it. It grew in intensity and then disappeared.

Hmm...that was odd.

"Okay, picking up something in here now. Let's head to the basement and work our way up, Jess." Megan waved her handheld device around looking for anomalies in the electromagnetic field. "Yes, definitely getting some spikes." She reached for her walkie-talkie and called the van, as if they couldn't see us on camera. "Okay, Mike? Becker? We're heading through the kitchen and to the basement. Getting some good spikes in here. Look at this, point four, point five and rising!"

"Why don't you hang out there for a few minutes? See what else you get."

"Got it," she said as she waved her gadget around. I closed my eyes and "felt" around the room. I gasped as whatever was in here quickly darted out. It was heading for the basement too! Then the pain came back. I grimaced and clutched my side.

"What is it, Jessica? You feeling something?" Megan touched my arm, genuine concern on her face.

"Yeah, I've got this pain in my side. It's coming and going."

"What kind of pain? Are you hurt, or is this some sort of transference?"

Transference. That was a good word for it. I could hardly think of how else to describe it. "I'm not sure yet. I'll keep you posted."

"Okay, well, let me know if it gets too bad. I don't want you to put yourself in danger."

In danger...

"Did you hear that?" James asked. He'd been on two investigations with us and had never intervened until now. He didn't move out from behind the camera, but I could see his puffy face was sweating. I felt sorry for the guy. He was never going to last in this business if he didn't get in better shape.

"Yeah, I heard it," I replied. I pulled the digital voice recorder out of my pocket. "Why don't we do a session, Megan? Before we go to the basement."

"What did you guys hear?" she asked. "I thought I heard a whisper. I assumed it was you."

"Nope, wasn't us," James and I answered simultaneously.

"Okay, let's do a session. I'll sit here. Jess, you go first."

I cleared my throat and waited for a moment. It was always nerve-wracking thinking about what to say. "We know you are here. We heard you speaking to us. Do you want to talk to me or to Megan?"

I remembered to count to five in my head before I asked another question. The audio recorder was my favorite tool for ghost hunting. It picked up voices that the human ear often missed. Except we had heard the voice just a minute ago. Maybe we wouldn't need the recorder in here.

"My name is Jessica, and this is Megan." I counted to five again in my head. I heard something that sounded like a bag of flour sliding across the floor.

"Did you..." I began to ask, but Megan interrupted with a nervous laugh.

"Yes. Keep talking. We're getting some action now. I guess they didn't want to stay hidden after all." She grinned as she looked around the room. "Do you know where that was coming from?"

"I think the doorway there, the one that goes from the kitchen to the basement."

Megan hopped up and opened the door. "Like someone was dragging something down the stairs?"

Nodding, I walked to stand beside her. For some reason I felt like there might be safety in numbers. I mean, we had been warned. We were in danger. "Did you just make that noise? We can hear you."

After a few seconds, I asked, "Can you make another noise? I know it takes a lot of energy, but speak really loudly this time." I waited another few seconds, then Megan and I gasped as we felt a breeze blow past us down the stairs.

"Is the front door open?" Megan asked James. He looked behind him and shook his head. "Okay, so the door is not open. The air conditioning and heating units have been turned off. I don't see any windows open in here. I can't imagine what that could be."

"Might be a window open down there. Or a door."

To another world. A dark world where you don't want to go. I kept that thought to myself.

Megan agreed and called down the stairs, "We are coming down now." Suddenly the pinch in my side returned, and I gasped at the sudden pain. "Oh yeah, that's not a normal pain. Definitely transference." Sometimes I felt the pain of others, and on a few occasions it had helped us figure out what happened to the ghostly occupants of the houses we visited. Most of the time there was no way to prove what I felt, but I believed the messages were accurate. At least in the case at the Halloran Hotel, we were able to prove it. Enid Halloran had died of blunt force trauma, which explained the almost debilitating head pain I experienced during last year's investigation. The older I got, the worse these episodes became. And now I was twenty-five. Would I live to be thirty? I couldn't imagine exploring haunted houses all my life. I would most certainly not enjoy it if I needed to be on pain medicine.

"Hold on to me, Jessica." Megan pulled out her tiny yet powerful flashlight and waved it on the steps in front of us.

After a few seconds the pain lessened but didn't completely vanish. "Can you hear that?" I asked as we descended. I could have sworn I heard someone crying. No, that was whimpering.

"I don't hear anything." We stood in silence with James on the stairs behind us. Megan clutched my hand now. That was a sure tell that she was "feeling" something. I was glad it wasn't just me. "Dang, it's cold down here. Is this normal?"

We moved into the space and spread out. James followed Megan as she waved her device. "Getting some major spikeage. Jess, how are you feeling? Anything else? Can you hear or see anything?"

The pain hit me so hard I nearly doubled over. I felt the sudden urge to cry for help as I fell to my knees.

"Oh my God! James, get Jessica." Megan pushed a button on the walkie-talkie and shouted, "Mike, get in here. Jessica needs help!" Then the tapping began.

Bang. Bang. Bang.

It was steady and growing louder. I could hear it, but I couldn't be sure they could. The pain increased in intensity, and I nearly gagged. "Where is that coming from? James, don't you dare leave us down here."

"I'm trying to get a wider shot. I see something!"

I pushed up from the ground and managed to sit cross-legged still holding my side. What was this feeling? A gunshot? A stab wound? Someone had definitely been hurt here, a woman, and she wanted her mother.

"Talk to me, Jessica."

"There's a woman here. She's over there." I pointed furiously at the far wall. As I did, the ghost slid back into the wall and an expression of terror crossed her face. She began to fade before my eyes. I gasped at the sight, and the pain began to subside. "Oh no! She's in the wall! She's in the wall! Get me something!" The banging grew louder, and I could hear footsteps upstairs. It had to be Becker and Mike. They ran down the stairs, but as soon as Mike's foot hit the basement floor the banging stopped.

"Jessica? Oh no, she's passed out."

But I wasn't passed out. I was still with them, in the in-between place where dreams and consciousness met.

And that was where they were. The two women: one younger and one older. Both with long, unbrushed hair, torn clothing and dirty hands.

Hands that had been digging for centuries to get out. I could see the younger woman quite plainly—she wanted me to see her. And I could see the wound, the black, bloody wound that was evidence of her horrific demise. As I watched in terror, unable to move as she reached for me, her long fingers extended to supernatural lengths and gripped my arm. Her pale face glowed and then vanished, revealing the bone underneath it.

"No!" I screamed in terror. Whether she meant to hurt me or not, I did not want her to touch me. But now she was leaning closer. Her fetid breath again filled my nose.

With a dry, dusty voice she said, *"Find me..."* She squeezed my wrist once more before she released me. Again I screamed, unable to verbalize what I saw. Mike and Becker lifted me off the cold floor as I writhed. I was fully awake now, and I let them carry me outside.

Mike's voice shook, even as he tried to remain controlled. "Jessica. Are you with me? Stop filming, James. Grab my phone! We need a doctor."

I found my voice and squeezed his hand. "No. I'm fine."

"The hell you are. Look at your skin...it's red." He held my arm gingerly and stared at my wrist. "What happened?"

"She wants out. She's in the wall, Mike. They are both in the wall! We have to get them out!"

That wasn't what he expected to hear. He rubbed his hand across his shaved head and put his arm around me as I sobbed. "Come on. Let's get you in the van."

"Please, we can't leave them in there." I leaned on his shoulder.

"It's okay, Jess. It's going to be all right. That's a wrap, guys. We'll meet in the morning."

Megan joined us long enough to glare at me, but I couldn't do anything but cry. Mike held me and carried me to the MHP van.

As I clung to him, I glanced back at the house once more. That's when I saw him, the other one. He'd stayed hidden most of the night, but he was there. Watching us.

Watching everything.

Watching and waiting.

Chapter Nine – Summer

"What the frick, Avery?" I gasped as my cousin nearly tripped over me. "What the heck are you doing running around in the dark? And what happened to the lights?"

"Summer? What are you doing here?"

I crossed my arms and looked at her like she was crazy. Did I need her permission to show up here? Hadn't *she* called *me* looking for a housekeeper? Needless to say, I didn't say that. "You called me all freaked out. Remember? Now what's going on?"

"We heard a big boom, and Jamie saw someone in the upstairs hallway. The lights just went out." Avery clutched my arm, and I could feel her shaking.

"You two. Get a grip, y'all. The big boom was probably thunder. It's about to storm, and it looks like it will be a doozy."

"I've heard storms before, and that was no storm," Detective Richards barked back.

I rolled my eyes. "Well, how do I know what it was? Maybe it was a power surge. That happens a lot in old houses like this. Let's go check the breaker box. It's in the basement, scaredy-cats."

"It can't be that," Richards snapped. "I've never heard a breaker box sound like breaking glass. It was nothing like a power surge. Nothing like that at all."

"Fine. It was a big scary ghost. Now give me that flashlight so I can check the box. Some detective," I said with a bleak laugh. I walked back through the kitchen and opened the basement door. I hated this basement, but it was nothing like the one at Sugar Hill. That basement felt horrific and always had a bad smell to it. Even though the air was dank here, it wasn't smelly and there were no rodents clawing at the walls trying to rip off my flesh. I accidentally kicked an ill-placed cardboard box, then walked over it and opened the panel. Sure enough, the main breaker had been flipped.

"Hold this a sec?" I handed Avery the flashlight and used both hands to flip the switch up. It was stubborn and didn't want to flip back into place, but it did eventually obey me. Naturally the brave detective hung back and didn't offer to help. Some hero. And of course, the lights came on. "See?"

Avery's blue eyes clamped on me. "I know we heard something. It sounded like glass breaking or maybe a chandelier crashing to the floor. And what about the person Jamie saw upstairs?"

"I bet I have the answer to that. Follow me."

We walked back up the basement stairs, and I closed and locked the door behind me. I always locked the one at Sugar Hill. "Come on, y'all. I'll show you the ghost."

"Mock me if you want to, but I saw someone up there. Maybe a transient. Someone looking for shelter from the storm? I don't know. I never said it was a ghost," Richards grumbled as he followed me up the wide staircase. As if it wanted to prove me right, the thunderstorm broke loose over us. The sound of thunder shook the walls of Thorn Hill and set the glass chandeliers tinkling as we arrived on the second floor.

"Welcome to Alabama, y'all. Home of big, scary thunderstorms at all times of the year." I couldn't help but smile at them. Sure, Avery had something to be afraid of, but I was pretty sure it wasn't this thunderstorm. And I seriously doubted if the family ghost would reveal himself to Jamie Richards. But then again, I was no expert. I wasn't even the "anointed one."

"I know I saw someone, Miss Dufresne."

"Please call me Summer. And I don't doubt you saw something. Was it that?" I pointed down the hall as I flicked on the light. There at the far end, standing between two suites, was the marble statue. I always hated that thing. That was an odd place to put a statue, but this was an odd house, no question about that. "I'd like you to meet Champion Dufresne and his dog, Spider. Champion was the son of Chase and Athena—their eldest son, to be more precise. He lived here from about 1835 to right before the War. In fact, he became something of a recluse. He shot himself dead cleaning his gun."

Richards looked relieved. He was one good-looking man, and except for being a little jumpy tonight, he seemed like a decent guy. Kind of the all-American type. Probably used to women falling all over him. I squinted as I appraised him, hoping he didn't realize how intimately I was assessing him. He was probably a reasonable lover, and I had no doubt he'd like to please Avery up one side and down the other. Although he hadn't yet. How did I know? It sure wasn't because my cousin confided in me. It was just that Richards had the "I'm-so-hungry-I-could-eat-a-bear" look. Surely Avery wasn't pining over Jonah Blight. No, I couldn't imagine that. Not at all. What a jerk that guy was!

With surprising jealousy, I wondered if Avery had seen the Lovely Man. If she'd lost her desire for a flesh-and-blood man. If Ambrose had come to her. If he'd kissed her and claimed her as his own as he once did me? I stole a peek at the ring, as if that would tell me what I wanted to know. It told me nothing. The silver ring with the rubies only served as a pretty reminder that I had been rejected by him. And by my family.

I wondered how this would all turn out. If she liked Richards at all, she should end the relationship now. Or else plan his funeral. Avery caught me staring at the ring and met my gaze knowingly. With an understanding smile she said, "Thanks for ghost busting for us, Summer. It's a relief to know the place is not haunted."

I couldn't let her off that easy. She needed to be cautious. And I felt my natural mean streak rising. "Oh, I didn't say the house wasn't haunted. I'm just saying that statue would freak anyone out—even if you knew it was there. And I knew it was going to storm tonight."

"I could sure use a drink," Richards said, licking his lips. I suddenly had the urge to kiss them. Strange, since I'd had Becker just a few hours ago. Two men in one night? That was too much, even for me.

"I think we all could. There's a liquor cabinet in the downstairs front room." We silently walked down the stairs together. I quickly led them to Susanna's room and poured us all Irish whiskey on the rocks. Avery sipped hers, but Richards didn't waste any time with his. I poured him another and sat on the sofa beside Avery.

The storm rolled over us. The lights flickered a few times, but we didn't talk for a while. Avery silently mused over Susanna's portrait and finally finished her drink. "She was so beautiful," she whispered as she put the glass down. Richards agreed and asked who she was.

M.L. Bullock

"Susanna Dufresne, former wife of Chase Dufresne. His left-hand wife. She lived here after they split up sometime around 1820."

"Left-hand wife? You mean mistress? I didn't think people did that sort of thing back in the old days." Richards stared up at the colorful painting. He squinted a bit as if he needed a good pair of glasses. I guessed like most macho types he didn't want to admit that failing.

"Well, people are people no matter what time they live in. And yes, they did separate. Some folks say they divorced, although it wasn't something that a proper person would speak about openly." *Why does this guy seem so familiar? Like I've met him somewhere before. That isn't possible. Is it?* The curve of his lips did seem familiar. I found myself once again thinking about kissing them.

"It was a sordid story. Apparently she was unfaithful to him, with his cousin no less, and he married Athena. And a lot of good her beauty did Susanna. It isn't always a blessing, is it?" I asked Avery.

She shook her head. "What happened to her? I mean, in the end? Do you know?"

"Have you finished Aunt Anne's videos?" I didn't want to talk about family matters in front of Richards, but the second glass of whiskey had warmed my heart and loosened my tongue. It wasn't like he was going to mention any of this to anyone. Anyone with a brain could see he was completely smitten with Avery. Or was it her money and prestige he was after? I felt a twinge of jealousy, but it didn't last long. I didn't really want to be matrone. Not really. It cost too much.

"No. Not yet."

"You should. She tells Susanna's story way better than I ever could, but I do know that the end of Susanna's life was very different from the beginning. She was a survivor."

"That's good to know."

Richards didn't interrupt us but just listened intently. Retrieving the whiskey bottle from the mahogany cabinet, he set it down on the coffee table. Avery pushed her glass toward him, and he filled it halfway. Again his movement seemed so familiar. I had to have met him somewhere before. The way he moved as he poured his drink. The way he slouched back and watched us. Yes, he liked to watch. *That also feels recognizable.*

Avery pleaded, "Tell me what you know. Tell me about Susanna and Chase...and tell me about...Ambrose."

My heart leaped at hearing his name mentioned aloud. Clearly Avery did not realize that just saying his name could be considered an invitation. Or that's what the old ladies in our family always warned. I'd tried it, and it hadn't worked for me. I *wanted* to summon him, but he never came when I called. Just then, I felt cold fingers on my neck as if someone were standing behind me, touching me. I shifted in my seat and glanced around, then snuggled back down against the pillow. No one was there, of course. What to tell her?

"I'm not sure your guest wants to hear about our family drama," I said with a laugh as I played with my ice cubes.

"It's hardly drama if it was that long ago, is it?" Richards said. "It's just history now. Besides, I would like to hear more about the Dufresne family history."

"I'm not sure you'd believe it all, Detective."

"Try me. I think it would be interesting. It's not many people who claim to know their lineage like you ladies. The Richards family is made up of criminals, I'm afraid. Well, except me. I at least didn't go into the family business."

"Which was?" I grinned at him, hoping to hear more about his criminal ancestry.

"Bootlegging, gambling and a few other things I wouldn't want to confess to."

I laughed at his soft disclosure. He wanted us to know some of the truth but not all of it. Reed already knew everything there was to know about Detective

Jamie Richards, from his grades in elementary school to his criminal record. If I wanted to know, I could.

"That sounds intriguing!" Avery said with a playful smile. "I always knew you were not what you seemed." I smiled too. I wondered if she really knew how true those words were. And if he thought his family tree was naughty, he really ought to see ours. It was full of adulterers, adulteresses, murderers, thieves and so much more. Maybe I'd scare him just for the fun of it.

"You know, there are scarier places than this old house or Sugar Hill. You should visit the Ramparts, or what's left of them, up on Clovis Road. That place will have you seeing things. They can't even build up there. We've tried, believe me. The Dufresne family owns all that now. Can't do a thing with it. It's all very hush-hush. Just ask Reed if you don't believe me."

"That's near here, right?"

"Yeah, you know it?" I asked him with a raised eyebrow.

"Yes, I saw the sign." Lying made him flush. Well, at least he was an easy read. He eagerly moved the conversation in another direction. "What's so scary about it?"

No sense in interrogating him now. The truth was there were no signs pointing to the Ramparts or Clovis Road. That stretch of land overlooking Mobile Bay had been abandoned long ago. I wasn't joking about the 'can't build there' part. Too many ghosts there. It was a terrible place. I'd been a few times, and that was enough to know I never wanted to go back. At least not at night. No, I take that back. Never. I never wanted to go back there. Teresa May got herself lost there once, and when they finally found her she was a blubbering mess. She hadn't been right since, and that was ten years ago.

Avery added, "You'd think the city, county or state government would want to remember that place. Honor all those who lived there. Maybe we should look into that?"

"I don't know, Avery. It's not a happy place. You could cut down all the trees and there would still be shadows there. I guess you've heard about the fire. The one that burned the Ramparts down to the ground; it was so hot a blaze that it burned the stones of the courthouse. They say Susanna set that fire and killed her lover, but he didn't die. He came back for her."

And all her descendants.

"What?" She gawked at me in surprise. "Why would she do that?"

"It was quite the scandal back in the day. She got her revenge for the wrong he did her."

"Wrong? What wrong?" Richards asked, looking from me to Avery. My pretty cousin was completely captivated by my story. *So she had seen Ambrose.* I wondered how much she knew. Poor Detective Richards. Nobody answered him.

Avery touched his hand and licked her perfect pink lips. "It's a long, sad story. Please go on, Summer."

"Shortly before the fire, Chase died under mysterious circumstances, and then Susanna set the fire."

Avery shook her head and pursed her lips. "I can't believe Susanna would do something like that. It just doesn't seem like her."

"How would you know, Avery? You can't believe everything Grandmother Margaret said—or Aunt Anne, for that matter. Things are rarely what they seem in this family. That's a tip that might help you later." My phone buzzed in my pocket. I didn't expect to hear from anyone tonight. A call this late could only mean something bad. Huh, this was unexpected. It was my most recent boy-toy, Becker. I picked up and put on my best bored voice. "Hey. You guys wrapped up already?"

"We had to shut down the investigation. Jessica, our psychic-medium, freaked out in your basement."

I slapped my forehead in disbelief. "What do you mean freaked out? Is she hurt?"

"Not physically, but you might want to stop by."

"On the way." I hung up the phone. Everyone had heard what Becker said. If I'd wanted to keep it a secret, I should have turned the volume down or stepped outside. But there was no help for that now.

Avery was on her feet and ready to roll. "We're coming with you."

"I can't stop you. It's your house," I replied with an extra bit of nonchalance.

"Summer, for the last time, this is *our* family and *our* family home. Right?"

"Sure." I popped up from the couch ready to see what havoc the ghost hunters had wreaked on Sugar Hill.

"Hey, I mean it." Avery grabbed my hand.

"I know you do." With rare impulsiveness, I hugged her. "Why do you have to be so nice, Avery? Everything would be much easier if I didn't like you." With that I walked quickly down the sidewalk and hopped in my car.

Tears filled my eyes as I drove back to Sugar Hill. This was bad. All of it. I didn't want to like Avery. I didn't want to let her walk into the trap that was prepared for her. I didn't want any of this to happen.

But it was all out of my hands.

Chapter Ten – Avery

"That is one weird girl," Jamie said as he opened the car door for me.

"She's my cousin and the closest thing I have to a sister, Jamie. Please don't call her that." I watched Summer's car lights disappear down the driveway.

"Sorry."

I prided myself on being good at reading people. For all her toughness and her show of independence, I knew that Summer was neither of those things. There was a deep emotional well hidden there. She had a keen intelligence, like her brother, but she kept it hidden and was comfortable hanging out in the shadows away from the spotlight. Despite what some might believe, I saw myself in her in some ways. Even America's Newscaster had to play down her smarts from time to time. Whether or not Summer would welcome my observation or my help, I wanted to help her succeed. She had a cooking show on the web, but so far we'd not talked about it. It had been a long time since anyone had needed me.

Jamie quietly got in the car and buckled up, an unsure look on his face. I felt like such a heel. "Hey, I don't mean to snap your head off, Jamie. You made the long drive here today, and now I've got you running the roads again. You must wonder what you've gotten yourself into." The thunder rolled overhead, but as of yet no rain hit the ground. This kind of storm, the kind with no rain, was what Vertie called an empty promise—and a bad omen. If she were here with us, she'd be humming a little tune against "haint" magic. I tried to remember the tune, but for the life of me I couldn't.

"And I didn't mean to offend you, Avery. I don't dislike Summer. Heck, I hardly know her, but I won't lie; I get the feeling she's not quite genuine. And that's on purpose. Maybe I'm just jaded. I've been a cop for too long."

"I will agree with you in one regard—Summer isn't very open with her feelings."

"That's not exactly what I meant."

"I get it. Believe me I do. But she's my family, and I want to help her."

"How will you help her? And do you think she wants your help?"

How could I explain to him the pain of being cut off from your family? To lose the people you love in one fell swoop to a freak accident? I knew that feeling. It was a loss that couldn't be explained to anyone. You had to feel it. Summer had been groomed for the role of matrone all her life. Reed hinted more than once that everyone assumed she would inherit the ring, but she hadn't. For a reason I had not yet discovered, Summer hadn't met Miss Anne's mysterious standard. Now I had what Summer wanted, and to be honest I felt bad about it. I felt guilty, and I'd learned a hard lesson with Amanda. Make sure your friends stay your friends.

"I don't have all the answers, Jamie." What else could I say?

He concentrated on driving and smiled apologetically. "Again, I'm sorry for saying she was weird. I don't express myself too well, or so I've been told."

"Really? Who told you that?"

"My ex-wife, Evelyn. She always wanted to put me on her couch."

"What?" I laughed. I suspected he'd been burned by love in the past, but I had no idea he'd been married. "What does that mean?"

"Oh, not like that. She's a psychologist now. Thanks to my kind monetary gift."

"I see."

"I never meant to keep my divorce a secret. It just never came up, and I'd rather forget those two years."

"A divorce is not a big deal to me, Jamie. Honestly. You met Jonah. No way your ex-wife could ever top him. But I have to ask, just to be sure, do you have any other deep, dark secrets you want to keep hidden? Any skeletons in the closet, Detective Richards?

Any children?" To my surprise, his tanned face turned red.

"No. Nothing like that. Just a dog that I surrendered. And I wouldn't say it's a secret...I've been meaning to tell you. You see, I used to live here, in this area, in Belle Fontaine."

"Really? Small world." The hairs on the back of my neck crept up. "When did you move to Atlanta?"

"After I graduated from high school. I had a friend who joined the police academy, and I tagged along. Fell in love with life in the big city."

"I know that feeling."

"The thing is, my childhood was kind of challenging. I couldn't remember large portions of it. Not for quite a while."

"A man of mystery...way to entice a girl."

"Evelyn called it 'childhood amnesia.' Something to do with trauma, but I think that's just psycho-speak."

"Might be some truth to it. I don't know much about psychology." That wasn't quite true. Ten years after my parents died, I was still seeing a therapist. It wasn't until I graduated college that I gave up those shrink sessions and threw myself into my career. Maybe I should have kept up with them.

"I can't say for sure. I couldn't remember a damn thing, though. That is, until I met you."

"Me?" Now I had the cold chills.

"It's the strangest thing. Like our meeting was some kind of switch or trigger." He laughed at the idea, like any of this was funny. "Now I sound like my ex-wife." Seeing that I wasn't amused he added, "I'm getting bits and pieces of memory, and the weird thing is, I think I remember you."

"That's wild. Did we know one another as children? We never lived here in Belle Fontaine, so I don't know how that would have happened. My father was in the military, and we traveled all throughout my childhood. I didn't settle down in Atlanta until Vertie and I moved there."

"Maybe we didn't. I don't know how to describe what I'm experiencing. It's like having this sense of déjà vu all the time. Like that street right there. I see it and recognize it from earlier, but I also remember when it wasn't there. I remember this road and how it used to be dirt and nothing but trees along both sides. There was also a meadow there and a large stream just beyond. I think I fished in it. I remember the sounds of cows lowing and the calling of the men who worked in those fields. I remember it all. And I can't tell you how or why." Jamie pulled the car over to the side of the road. "But that's only been happening since you and I have gotten...close."

There wasn't any traffic, and I suddenly felt very isolated. Good things didn't happen to me in cars.

"What are you doing?"

"I have to tell you everything. My mother, she was related to the Dufresnes. Not closely, but there is a connection between us."

"Can't we talk about all this later? We have to go to Sugar Hill, Jamie."

"I know, but I can't wait another minute to tell you. You have to understand." Was he crying? He wiped at his eyes, which made me even more uncomfortable. His hands were shaking, and his voice dropped to a whisper. "I swear to you, I've been here before. In this car. With you. But it's not just that. I firmly believe I have been here before-before."

I shook my head in disbelief. What was he trying to say? Maybe this was why he was divorced. Was he mentally unbalanced? Was this expression some kind of metaphor that I wasn't getting? "I don't understand."

"Let me explain it another way. Until I met you, I never believed in past lives or living more than one life. But now I'm not so sure. Because that's the only thing that makes sense to me."

"I'm trying to follow." I glanced nervously over my shoulder, half hoping a car would appear behind us. Where was all the traffic?

"Since the first time I met you, I felt like you were special. Like I knew you."

"I hear that a lot. When people see you on their televisions night after night, they tend to feel that way. I think there's a name for that psychological effect. I don't mean to be insensitive, but I'd really like to get to Sugar Hill."

"I can tell by your expression that you think I'm certifiable. I was afraid of that." He leaned back in his seat and sighed heavily. "I don't know what I expected you to say, but I had to be honest with you. I can't keep this a secret anymore."

"I understand, Jamie." I had read somewhere that using the other person's name sometimes defused dangerous situations. I hoped it was true. "Try to look at this from my side. I don't want to think you would hurt me, but here I am, sitting on the side of the road, against my will."

"Against your will? Oh God, Avery! I would never hurt you! Never in a million years. I want to protect you. In fact, I believe I was sent here to protect you."

"Sent? By who?"

"I don't know. The Powers That Be? God? Whatever you want to call whoever is orchestrating all this."

"Jamie, I see this is important to you, but I can't focus on this right now. I have to know everyone is safe at Sugar Hill. Can we talk about this later tonight?" I slapped a fake smile on my face. I had my hand on the door handle now, just in case he said no. My skin was crawling, and the look in his eyes was different from any I had seen before.

Except once.

He was freaking me out. He didn't seem to hear me but just kept talking.

"And while I'm confessing, I have to tell you this."

"No, please don't. Save it for later."

He droned on as if I were mute. "I have told two other women that I loved them, and I believed I did when I said it but..."

"Jamie...now isn't..."

"Yes, I said 'I love you,' but that was nothing compared to how I feel about you. You have to understand." He grabbed my hands and stared into my eyes. I wanted to cry but couldn't allow myself to go there.

No, it's best to keep cool, I warned myself.

"I want to understand, Jamie." With every second that passed I was planning my escape.

You are my soul mate, Susanna.

"Wait? What did you say?"

"I was trying to say, although I'm not doing a very good job, that I love you. God! What am I doing? I should never have told you that. See? That right there should tell you something. I've never said it first." He laughed again, but it was a sick sound. He was lost in his own head and not really talking to me. It was as if he were trying to explain all this to himself. I was so upset I wanted to scream.

"Um, oh, that's so nice to hear, Jamie. I haven't heard that in forever. Although it is very early in our relationship, I can tell that you are special to me too and we have the potential to be something great together."

"Good. I just wanted to get that out there."

And then all the intensity in his voice was gone. It was as if he did not notice that he'd called me Susanna. Or that he'd told me he was my soul mate. He did not seem to notice that his behavior was beyond inappropriate and that I was not at all happy about this turn of events. He was himself again. I sat in the car staring straight ahead as we drove down the road in his classic Ford Mustang. The rain began to fall, and I covertly wiped at my eyes.

If I could just get to Sugar Hill, everything would be okay. *If I can just make it there I won't be alone.*

I prayed to God that I would make it.

PART THREE

Chapter Eleven – Avery

We arrived at Sugar Hill to find Reed and the crew of My Haunted Plantation practically mixing it up in the driveway. My cousin and one of the crew members, I assumed the guy in charge, were arguing like two kids totally oblivious to the rain that had finally begun to fall.

"You can't expect me to tear down walls on the word of a psychic. Do you have any proof that there is a body in there? If you do, I want to see it!"

"Sir, that's not what I'm saying. I'm just trying to make you see that it's a possibility. Jessica believes she saw something, and that's good enough for me."

Reed snorted. "Not for me."

"Hey, what's happening? Is Jessica okay?" I touched his shoulder hoping to calm the situation and get the hell away from Jamie. What a night this had turned out to be! Not at all what I had expected.

"These folks want me to tear down a basement wall because a ghost said there were bodies buried there. Can you believe this?" Reed was walking up and down the driveway, completely ignoring the rain. His black hair was wet yet somehow still wavy, and he was as angry as I'd ever seen him.

"Reed, let's get inside out of the rain and talk like civilized people."

"I don't want to have anything to do with this!" he whispered to himself. Or to me. I couldn't tell which.

"Well, that's a problem, isn't it? I need you to act like the family attorney. If there is even a remote chance that there is a body or two in the wall, it is our responsibility to deal with it all. So get it together, Reed." Why were all the men in my life losing their minds today?

"Fine."

We led the group of ghost hunters inside and gathered in the dining room. One of the housekeepers busily made coffee and poured iced sodas. Robin brought in warm towels and politely asked Reed if she needed to make up rooms for our guests.

I answered for him, "That would be lovely, Robin. Please do that, just in case someone wants to stay. It's raining cats and dogs, and we might be chatting a while. Summer and Jamie will need rooms for sure. Is Dinah here?"

"Last I saw her, she was upstairs...doing something. Most everyone else left, you know, to give the crew some space. Do you want me to go look for her?"

"No, that's not necessary. Thank you for staying and helping, Robin." She smiled and got back to handing out towels. I didn't know any of these people. Where was Jessica? I walked into the parlor and found her sitting on the floor with a soggy blanket wrapped around her. She stared out the window and didn't even appear to notice I was in the room.

"Jessica? There you are. Mind if I sit with you?" I waited, but she didn't move and barely blinked. "Jessica?" I wondered if it had been a mistake not to insist she go to the hospital for a checkup. She was calm and quiet. "May I sit with you?"

"Sure."

"Are you up to talking?" I sat on the floor next to her. This was strange, sitting on the floor of my own living room. I touched her shoulder reassuringly. "What did you see downstairs? You can talk to me, Jessica. I've seen things too."

She glanced over my shoulder at the boisterous gathering in the other room where Reed and Mike were still bickering. Jamie lurked nearby, but I didn't invite him closer. I didn't even look at him.

"Pay no attention to them. Tell me what you saw, Jessica."

Her blue eyes reflected her discomfort. "I felt a pain in my side before I saw anything. That has happened before, but not to this degree. It started as mild pain in my right side and steadily worsened. I could feel the blood pouring out of my body." She shivered uncontrollably as she spoke, so I pulled the gray blanket closer around her. Her eyes had dark circles under them; I'd seen those eyes before, during my tenure as an anchor at WBTV in Atlanta. They were eyes that had seen something horrible, like a house fire or the death of a loved one. I couldn't be absolutely positive, but I was confident that she believed what she was telling me was true.

"It was where he shot her, Avery." She sobbed, and I held her hand. "Her father shot her. Her name, her name...is Regina. I can hear her calling for help. She's calling her mother and screaming at her father. Then I hear pounding on the wall. Like she wasn't quite dead after all."

"What else did you see, Jessica? What did this woman look like?"

"She was young, younger than us. She had long brown hair, and her dress was bloody. I can still hear the banging. Can't you hear it? The pounding on the walls, like a *boom, boom, boom*. The pounding. The crying. I hear the scratching—no! They aren't dead. And they scratch! They scratch to get out." Then she zoned out. She sat staring off into space like I wasn't even there.

"Jessica, can you listen to me?"

"Yes." She talked like someone who was in a trance or maybe in shock. Her voice sounded dreamy and soft, softer than normal, and she didn't move a muscle now. Had she hypnotized herself? A memory of a long-forgotten interview with a medium rattled around in my mind. Yes, if I remembered correctly, these psychics sometimes self-hypnotized in order to get a "better" signal. It almost seemed like she'd done that. What if she was stuck? *Too bad Jamie's ex-wife wasn't here to give us a diagnosis,* I thought sourly.

I'd interviewed a hypnotist once and even sat through a demonstration of his abilities. Maybe I could use that experience now.

"Jessica, I know you want to help her, but it's time to shut it off. You can't stay tuned into that other world like that. It's not good for anyone. Let's try this. I am going to count backwards from three, and when I get to one, you are going to feel like yourself again. You won't be afraid anymore." I added quickly, "But you will remember everything. Ready?"

She whimpered as she held the cup of tea, her eyes open. "Yes, I am ready."

"Three, two, one. Now wake up." I snapped my fingers, and she brightened instantly.

"Avery?" She smiled at me all silly, like she had a bit of a buzz.

"Hi, girl. How are you feeling?"

"Never better." She smoothed her hair and glanced around the room. I could tell she was trying to put two and two together. That wasn't a good sign. I had hoped she would recall our conversation. But then again, I really didn't know what the heck I was doing.

"I can't be sure, but I think you were in a trance of some sort. You feel okay now?"

"Just great. I am hungry, though."

"Good! We will get you something to munch on. But first tell me what you saw."

"When?" She sipped her tea now and stared at me with wide eyes. The smudges under them had vanished.

"In the basement."

"Yes, that place is weird." She screwed up her face trying to remember what she saw, when someone brought in a tray of sandwiches and offered her one. "Oh look, there are some sandwiches."

Well, this hadn't gone exactly as planned. "Enjoy your snack; I'm going to talk with Reed for a minute. I'll come back to check on you."

"All right." Jessica ate her food with zeal, and I could hardly believe the change in her.

I didn't realize that Reed had been watching all this. When I turned around, he was behind me. "Reed, they can't keep investigating here. It is far too dangerous. They need to go."

"Yes, but they have a signed contract, so they have a right to be here. Remember? I didn't call them out here."

"What about the bodies? Are there bodies in the basement?"

"Not as far as I know, but I have a friend from the local university who works in the anthropology department. I told him what happened here, and he is going to help us. He also thinks the whole thing is ridiculous, that the chances of skeletons being hidden in the walls are slim to none. But he has a machine that can detect anomalies in houses and caves and whatnot. He's promised to come out tomorrow and wave his 'magic wand' in our basement. If there are bones in there we will know it, but I think it's plain that this has all come from the imagination of a very disturbed young lady."

"I'm not so sure. I have seen Grandmother Margaret's videos. So much has happened in this house. So much death and loss. And what about the fact that Jessica called the girl Regina. That was Chase Dufresne's sister! She and her mother died while he was in New Orleans. Maybe they died here."

"Whoa, Avery!" He glanced around at the eyes that were watching us now. "I think you are getting way ahead of yourself on this." I felt my exasperation rising, but I let him go on. "Avery, you were an investigative reporter. Would you even report on this with this kind of evidence?" Robin popped back in and offered us coffee. We both refused, and Reed walked into the second parlor room and waved for me to follow him.

Yeah, he's right. There wasn't much to go on except feelings and a paranormal investigator who didn't seem to have it all together.

"Avery, I promise, if we find anything there, we will do what's right. But for now, let's calm the situation. I think it's best that we keep them out of the house. At least temporarily. Having this investigation appear on television would be bad for all of us."

"I want to be here when the search is done. I want to know."

"Okay, but let's keep this between us. If the board heard, they would flip out for sure! They'd replace me and if they could they would replace you too. For now, let's keep this as quiet as possible. Tell your boyfriend to keep quiet too."

"He's not my boyfriend," I said nervously, "and I think something is wrong with him."

"Really? What do you mean?" I pretended that I didn't see the smirk on his face.

"This place, it affects everyone, doesn't it? What's going on here, Reed?" I could tell that struck a nerve. "You know what's going on and you aren't telling me. And Thorn Hill—it's the same way. It's like the past isn't really in the past."

Reed shoved his hands in his pockets and walked to the window. He looked through the curtains as if he were worried someone would hear us. "Is the past ever really in the past? There are experiences that transcend time, Avery. Promises that must be kept. Surely you feel that. You understand that."

"I don't know that I do. I want so badly to figure it all out, but I haven't. Not yet."

Reed grabbed my hands and pulled me close. "You will. One day you will wake up and it will all make sense. I promise."

I breathed a sigh of relief. I wasn't sure that I believed him, but it felt good to hear him say it. Then to my complete surprise he kissed me. And I didn't resist. I didn't want to. His lips were strong and warm. I breathed him in as we pulled away, only a few inches apart. He smelled like fresh rain and sandalwood. He touched my face and stepped back. Unsure what the heck to do, I decided I had to get away.

Away from everyone.

I walked quickly out of the room and up the stairs. I thought I heard Summer call me, but I didn't answer. I sped to my room and locked the door like a guilty teenager. Fortunately, nobody came knocking. Feeling that one room wasn't enough to separate me from the world, I went into the bathroom, turned on the faucets and quickly shed my clothes. I slipped into the water, which made my skin tingle as the blood began to flow again. I hadn't realized I'd gotten so cold. I soaked for a long time and stared out the big picture window. The water slid down the panes in rivulets, and watching it calmed me.

I noticed my hands were beginning to prune, so I quickly dried off, changed into my pajamas and lit the fireplace. After a while, I stopped thinking about the kiss. I became drowsy and managed to climb into bed. My phone rang a few times, but I didn't answer it. I didn't even look to see who called.

I slipped off into a dream where Reed showered me with tender kisses and I melted in his arms like warmed honey. Then it wasn't Reed I kissed—it was Jamie. Not the crazy Jamie but the confident detective I had fallen for in Atlanta. I practically cried with relief.

Yes, he was the one I should be with! We kissed more fervently, more passionately. Our hands were all over one another.

And then it wasn't Jamie anymore—it was Ambrose.

Ambrose with his dark eyes and his spicy scent. Ambrose with his rough hands and his lips that warmed my skin and set my senses alight. He stirred something dormant in me, made me want more of him.

This was a dream, wasn't it? Who would see me? Who would know that I kissed him back? I kissed him with all my might. I whispered his name, uncaring who heard me.

I surrendered myself to him and fell back on the bed; I wasn't naked, but the feeling of silk surrounded me. Then the man I kissed was no longer Ambrose but Chase. Chase kissed me and pulled at my clothes. He held me in his arms, kissed my neck and tenderly kissed my body. I wasn't wearing my pinstriped pajamas now but a blue silk gown that he quickly unlaced. I was so confused, I could not fight him.

Suddenly, he was inside me. Chase was making love to me, and pleasure washed over me. Yes, all I wanted was Chase.

Chase, my love! Chase, my own darling! Chase, I want to lose myself in you!

My hands flew into his hair, and I kissed his lips and looked into those bright eyes. And then he was Chase no longer but Ambrose again. Dark and demanding. He gave no pleasure but only took his. And strangely, there was pleasure in that too.

"Stop, Ambrose! No! I don't want you! I want Chase!"

Then someone was shaking me. Shaking me hard, straddling me and forcing my hands down above my head. I looked up into the face of Susanna and began to cry.

"What...just...happened...to me, Susanna? I think I am going...crazy. Please help me. I have to leave this place."

"We cannot leave. We can never leave. We are his now. The ring is the proof. *You are his soul mate.*"

"No!" I screamed and twisted my body to get away. Then Susanna vanished and I became aware that I was only dreaming. I shook myself awake and sobbed in the darkness. I pulled the covers tighter around me and realized that I was not alone.

Jamie was sleeping beside me, naked and sweating. And we must have made love, for I was also naked and covered in sweat.

But I had not made love to Jamie. I made love to Chase—or was it Ambrose? Hadn't I locked the door before I went to bed?

What was happening?

Chapter Twelve – Jessica

Mike looked tired. We all did. This ghost hunt had really been a letdown. Or more specifically, I had been a letdown. I'd let the team down with my "antics," Megan said.

Maybe I'd had a panic attack or something? The team watched the video together, and it was like I was watching a stranger. It was my voice, my face, yet I didn't remember any of it after coming down the stairs. It wasn't like me to act like a rookie. I'd been working in the paranormal field for four years, and before that I was seeing ghosts in my parents' old barn. As far back as I could remember, I'd been seeing ghosts, feeling them. Many of those experiences had been downright frightening, like the man with the hatchet in his forehead and the gray girl who kept rising from the pond behind our old home. No one could compel me to swim in the water after seeing that.

I asked Mike to play the tape again and again, hoping to trigger some memory of what happened. I desperately wanted to get back into that basement, but it wasn't going to happen, all thanks to me. Even if I could persuade Avery to let me revisit the place, Reed Dufresne wasn't having any of it. And he warned us politely but sternly about reporting on what I had seen and heard. Who could blame him?

Megan shot me another dirty look, as if I hadn't understood the first dozen or so she'd already lobbed my way. *Oh, Megan. My on-screen fake friend. If only the world knew what a real hater you were.* Even though Mike had no interest in me romantically or I him, she couldn't stand the fact that someone else might garner any of his attention. Mike was crazy about Megan, although I wasn't sure why, but she was too blind to see it. Maybe if she spent less time swiping on makeup and spray-tanning herself she'd have better perception. But instead of dealing with her own issues, she chose to blame me for her problems.

Whatever! I'll get to the bottom of this myself.

Mike turned off the tape and gave the cameraman the signal that we were about ready to film our team meeting. Obediently, we leaned in around the table and listened intently as our leader officially filled us in on the next leg of our assignment.

"I met with Reed Dufresne this morning. He has invited us to hunt some of their other properties, and that's exciting. This is a once-in-a-lifetime chance, guys." Mike's cheerful attitude was infectious, and we followed his lead.

"That's excellent. Tell us what's up!" Megan piped in.

"Let me preface this by saying we have a real opportunity here to firmly show the world that the Gulf Coast is truly a hotbed of paranormal activity. Of course, anyone from the South would tell you they knew this already." We laughed along, and he smiled as if this were the best news ever. I noticed he carefully didn't mention my meltdown or the possibility of skeletons in the basement walls of Sugar Hill. I guessed Reed had had a few words with the Paranormal Channel too. "We'll finish our investigation at Sugar Hill before we leave, but for now let's take a look at some of these other locations." He spread a map on the table, and we all oohed and aahed over it.

"Some say a few of these hot spots are too dangerous for ghost hunting, but I know you guys aren't ones to run away from anything paranormal."

Becker interjected, "Hardly. They should know all that does is make us want to look at it harder."

Again we all chuckled, including James, who was sometimes scared out of his mind during assignments. "This is Thorn Hill. It's basically a replica of Sugar Hill, built by the same architect and around the same time."

"That's weird. Why would they want two of the same house?" I asked.

"It wasn't unusual in those days for a gentleman to keep two households."

"What?" Megan asked as she leaned back in her chair.

"It's true. It was legal at the time to have two wives. Not unlike other men, Mr. Dufresne kept one wife in one location and the other in another."

"The nerve of that guy. He'd never get away with that today," Megan said. Mike didn't take the bait. He kept his presentation professional and moved along quickly.

"And we have the home of the late Anne Dufresne—that's the Rose Cottage—and there is a wooded area just here called the Ramparts. That's where I'm leaning because there is so much history in that compact area. It hasn't been explored much because it is pretty treacherous. There's a short climb up the bluff—the road is basically washed out and goes out only so far. It's near the waterfront, close to where the slave ships unloaded. It began as a shanty town, but fortunes were made there and the place developed quite a reputation for having shops for just about anything you could imagine. Until someone burned it down."

"Burned it down? Who? Why?" Megan leaned forward a bit to give the audience a peek at her cleavage. Yes, she was one to make sure the camera stayed on her. I didn't care. I wanted to get on with the investigation and prove I wasn't a complete fruitcake.

"There are two main stories about that event. One story says that Susanna Dufresne, the cast-off wife of Chase Dufresne, lit the Ramparts on fire as an act of revenge against her unfaithful lover. The second rumor, and this one might have some truth to it, says Chase Dufresne's second wife, Athena, set the Ramparts ablaze herself in retaliation for Chase's murder. Athena blamed Susanna for his demise, and it was a well-known fact that she and Susanna were constantly at war with one another. Athena had tried for years to get Chase to divorce Susanna, and she greatly resented that her husband not only had another woman but was legally married to her."

"So this battle between the two women, that's probably the cause of the conflagration?" James asked. I was impressed with his vocabulary.

"Possibly. As I mentioned, Athena begged Chase to dissolve his relationship with Susanna, but he never gave in. When he died in 1825, most of the properties went to Susanna, so naturally Athena took her to court. After all, Susanna was a quadroon and not white."

"Get out of here!" Megan slapped her hand on the table. *Okay. Now somebody was going over the top.*

"The courts did not rule in Athena's favor, so she may have taken matters into her own hands."

I had to speak up now. Everyone had to participate in these on-camera pep rallies. "I say we investigate the Ramparts while the weather is clear. That sounds interesting, and I like the idea of an outdoor exploration. Might be better than haunting around old basements."

Megan cast me another uneasy look, and I couldn't help but smile at her. I didn't care if the camera picked up on that. I was tired of pretending we were pals. I was tired of fake ghost hunting too. I only signed on to this gig because I liked Mike and believed him when he said he was sincere in his search for the paranormal. I wasn't as sure now, but it was kind of too late. I had signed a contract. I couldn't quit. I had to keep going at least until the season ended next spring.

Becker stood up and tapped the map with his tattooed fingers, a big grin on his face, "Well, as they say in the movies, 'I ain't afraid of no ghosts.' I vote for the Ramparts."

Mike said, "I vote Ramparts, too. Megan? You in?"

"Yes! I love it. I think I'll do some research before we head out. Should we make a daylight trip first?"

"I think that would be wise. Let's find a few spots we can hone in on and focus our equipment there. I don't like the idea of you guys roaming around the woods in the dark."

"Aw, you're no fun," Megan said as she wrote down a few notes in her notebook. "You game for this, Jess?"

"Sure, but only if I get to hold my own flashlight." Megan had a tendency to forget to check the batteries on just about every electronic device she held. It wasn't a huge swipe at her, but as expected she took it as one.

"Ha, ha, ha," she answered playfully. "I can't help it if all power drains happen to you."

Everyone laughed at our "friendly" exchange. At least until the cameras stopped rolling.

Chapter Thirteen – Avery

The Rose Cottage had the feeling of spring, even though it was nearly November. The cottage was surrounded by evergreen trees including some fragrant cedars and neatly trimmed holly shrubs. Light green shutters and a pair of hearty palm trees in the front yard made me think of warmer days. Two large white rocking chairs decked out the front porch, and the front door was wide open. The screen door kept the mosquitoes out. You had to worry about them down here, even this time of year. It was a friendly picture of life at the Rose Cottage.

When I called Mitchell earlier this morning I had no real agenda—other than I needed to talk to someone. And since Miss Anne had trusted him, why shouldn't I? I'd managed to sneak into the bathroom and make the call before stepping into the shower. Somehow I did it all without waking Jamie. For that at least, I was grateful. As I washed away the memories of last night's bizarre dream, I wondered what I would say to him when I emerged. Why in the world had I slept with him? Did I even consent? I must have, since I'd locked the door—I had to have opened it for him! I wasn't going to accuse him of anything. I finally settled on, *"I'm sorry, Jamie, but this is too intense for me."* It was better than, *"I don't remember inviting you into my bedroom or making love to you. Get out before I press charges."*

I needn't have worried because by the time I got out of the shower he was gone. I buzzed Robin's intercom to verify it, and she reported that he had indeed left Sugar Hill. "No, he didn't mention where he was going and didn't stay for breakfast. Sorry, ma'am."

Relieved, I gave her my instructions for the day. "I'm going to leave for a little while, but I'll be back for lunch. If the My Haunted Plantation people return, you can allow them in, but keep them out of the basement. And no filming while I'm gone. Are there any other guests in the house?"

"No, ma'am. Everyone's gone."

That surprised me. "Is Summer still here?"

"I'm not sure. Would you like me to call her room?"

"No. That's okay. I'll see if she's in. Thanks." I flipped off the intercom and finished dressing quickly. I hated the idea of Jamie showing back up unannounced. A few broken images of making love with him last night surfaced in my mind. What really happened?

I can't think about this right now.

I decided it was a blue jeans kind of day. Before I moved to Belle Fontaine I didn't even own a pair. *My, how things have changed.* I slid on a purple sweater and my new boots, and I grabbed a jacket for the morning chill. I decided not to bring my purse, so I grabbed my keys, some cash and my driver's license. At the last minute I decided to take my cell phone but turned off the ringer. There was no one I wanted to talk to. Not Reed, not Jamie. Not even Summer.

As I walked down the stairs I noticed how empty Sugar Hill felt. That was different. It was as if someone had taken a broom and swept away all the spiritual debris. The eyes that bore down on me from the portraits weren't staring too intently today. The smiles on the busts of forgotten Dufresnes didn't display their familiar leers. Those stone faces were neither interested nor malicious-looking. These were the expressions of the proud, distant dead, not of lingering ghosts. They couldn't care less about the goings-on of the living. Nothing was on the landing above; no moving shadows like the ones that I frequently imagined slid down the wall behind me as I made my way down the stairs. I paused for a moment. It was here that I always had the sensation that someone was watching me or stalking close behind me. No. I felt none of that this morning. I simultaneously felt relieved and worried about the significance of it all.

Why had the house suddenly gone silent?

Maybe it was the same at Thorn Hill? I'd find out later today. I had to go back to retrieve my overnight bag. Or maybe I didn't. Was there anything in there I couldn't replace? *Oh, come on, you big coward.*

Before I eased the car out of the driveway I called Mitchell again. "Hey, this is Avery. I'm on the way now."

"Have you had breakfast?"

"No, but coffee is fine for me. Don't go to any trouble."

"See you soon."

Now here I was. Mitchell's large frame filled the doorway, and he welcomed me with a friendly smile. He seemed genuinely glad to see me alive and well. "Avery, come in." He glanced nervously at the driveway as if he expected someone else.

"It's just me, Mitchell."

He visibly relaxed. "Good. Come inside. I have fresh coffee."

"Perfect. What a beautiful cottage! You'll have to give me a tour."

We went inside, and Mitchell led me to the living room. It was not a very large room, but it had plenty of comfortable-looking seating and loads of embroidered pillows. Thriving green plants were positioned in places where they could take in some sun. My cousin had thoughtfully arranged some delicious-smelling croissants and an assortment of fruit on a tray. It was such a nice thought. He'd even put a fresh flower in a vase. The idea of Mitchell picking flowers for me was truly humbling. "Do these grow here? I noticed you have a hothouse."

"We do, but these are tea roses and I don't grow them. I haven't had much luck with roses, not yet, but I'm hoping to give it another try this spring. No, these I purchased from the supermarket." His confession made his cheeks flush. "I'm afraid the flower gardens are going to look horrible this spring without Aunt Anne to care for them." His voice caught as he spoke about her death, and she'd been gone for several months.

"I am sure you will get the hang of it." I glanced around the room, taking in the built-in bookcases loaded with books and interesting bird figurines. I wondered who the bird enthusiast was, Mitchell or Miss Anne? I sipped the coffee and put the china cup down on the saucer. Until I moved back home to Belle Fontaine, I rarely drank from proper cups and saucers. This was indeed a treat. "How are you, Mitchell? I haven't seen you at the house in ages. Is there anything I can do for you?"

"I have everything I need here, cousin. And I know how time-consuming managing the daily details is for someone who stays as busy as you. I wouldn't want to add undue pressure." He surveyed me, obviously curious as to the reason for my visit. What could I tell him? I wasn't sure myself.

"You aren't lonely here by yourself? You are always welcome to come visit me for a few days. You can stay at the house anytime you please—or at Thorn Hill."

"Why would I go there?"

"Haven't you heard? A television crew from a show called My Haunted Plantation has been at Sugar Hill. Before it's all said and done, they'll also investigate Thorn Hill."

He avoided eye contact and poured his coffee from the white teapot with the gold initials. It must have belonged to Miss Anne too. "I like being alone, and I have no plans to go to either Sugar Hill or Thorn Hill. In fact, I plan on asking Reed to find someone else to fill the board opening. That's one group I don't want to be part of—no offense."

"Oh. That was my idea, I'm afraid. But if it's not what you want, you don't have to. I am sure the board will come up with a name they can all agree on. For what it's worth, I'm not offended. But before you totally write off the idea, promise me you'll think about it a few days first?"

"I don't think I'd be much good on the board. Who's going to listen to me?" I had the distinct feeling that Mitchell was repeating someone else's assessment of him.

I leaned forward and clasped my hands. "Many people listen to you. I do! I want to trust Reed and your sister, but quite frankly, I always feel as if I am getting half the story from them." I chewed my lip and continued, "It's not that they are against me, but I feel like they aren't quite with me, if that makes sense. In many ways, I'm still an outsider. Even with my own family! I could use your help, Mitchell. If Miss Anne trusted you, then I should too."

He smiled at the mention of his favorite aunt. "I thank you for saying so, and I will do as you ask. I will think about it." He took another sip and offered me more coffee. I declined and leaned back in the comfortable seat.

"Mitchell, do you know what is happening at Sugar Hill? I have to know. I need a friend, and that's why I came to see you. I am surrounded by family, but I am not sure I can trust any of them." I grappled with what to say next. *Reed kissed me. I liked it. Summer not-so-secretly hates me. My boyfriend is a nut, and I'm dreaming about my ancestors in very inappropriate ways.*

Mitchell leaned back on the settee and stared at me intently. "So you know that things in our family aren't...right?"

"I do. Tell me what you know, Mitchell. Please, tell me what you know."

He turned blood red, and for a minute I thought he might ask me to leave.

"You know how much I loved Aunt Anne. She was the best human being I ever knew. She had such a heart for her family, even though they were all extremely ungrateful for all her care. I promised her that she could always trust me to keep her confidences. Even though she has passed on, I can't imagine breaking them now, even for you. It would be unkind to her memory. She made sure you had what you needed. She left you the video records and the other stuff, like Vertie's journals. That should tell you everything you need to know."

"Vertie's journals? I never received any journals."

"What?" He frowned. "I suppose Reed kept those back from you for his own reasons." I could tell there was no love lost between those two. "Well, you know about them now. You should insist that he give them to you immediately."

"And you can't tell me what's in them?"

"I never read them, Avery. And even if I did know anything, it is not my place to tell you. Aunt Anne kept the journals safe after Vertie's death, and they were intended to go to you. She wouldn't send them until you agreed to return home. I disagreed with her on that point, but she was one to keep her own mind on things."

"Why would she hold them back? Shouldn't I know what Vertie had to say? She was my grandmother!" I was growing angrier by the second, at Reed for keeping my property from me and denying me one last connection with Vertie, and at Anne. She had the answers to the ever-expanding puzzle of Sugar Hill, but she died with all her secrets and left me to interpret

Grandmother Margaret's mad ramblings by myself. And did I really have a choice? I woke up with this ring on my finger. A ring that wouldn't come off.

I halfheartedly tugged at the ring, but of course it didn't budge. "What about this ring, Mitchell? Why can't I take it off? What does it really mean? Reed tried to tell me it signified that the matrone was 'married' to the family, but that's just bull crap, isn't it?" I was on my feet now. The cordial tea party was forgotten, and I was ready to go to battle—I just wasn't sure with whom. Surely not with Mitchell and his sad puppy-dog eyes.

"Come on, Avery. Let's go for a walk." He rose from the striped settee, and I realized he almost had to duck to move around these rooms. The cottage had such low ceilings compared to the big airy spaces of Sugar Hill.

"A walk?"

"In Aunt Anne's gardens. I'll show you the hothouse. Grab your jacket, though; it's chilly in the back."

We walked along a brick pathway and enjoyed the cool weather in silence. Like any good reporter, I allowed him to lead the conversation, when he finally spoke. "Currently there are three major branches in our family. There are Vertie's children, Asner's children and Anne's. Summer and I are Asner's grandchildren."

"Wait. Vertie had only one child, Andrew, my father. Right?"

He glanced at me sadly and didn't speak again until we arrived at the hothouse. I couldn't wait to read Vertie's journals now.

"I see." I swallowed at the thought of another family secret to uncover. "And who are Anne's grandchildren?"

"Reed, Pierce and our two cousins, Meredith and Marguerite. But they died a very long time ago."

"But I thought Reed was Asner's child. How did I get that wrong? He's always calling her Aunt Anne. I just assumed..."

"She adopted him, but he is a Dufresne. That's another story for another time."

I couldn't believe it. I assumed Mitchell had a reason for telling me all this, but darned if I knew what that was.

He swung open the door to the massive hothouse, and the warmth immediately cheered me. He was right, the backyard was very chilly.

"Because you say you want to know what's going on, that's how you learn. You have to know who is married to whom. You have to know whose blood flows in your veins. And whose doesn't. You don't have anything if you don't have the right...alliance."

We shed our jackets, and he hung them on a wooden rack. Then he slid his hands into some tight gloves and handed me a pair. The gloves must have belonged to Miss Anne. Who else would have been out here? The gloves were cotton with a pretty floral pattern, and the fingers were slightly soiled. The smell of clean dirt comforted me, and I accepted a potted plant from him. He pointed at a small shovel and an empty row of dirt in a raised flowerbed. He had dozens of square flowerbeds in the hothouse. These were raised high off the ground, making it easier for him to tend to his floral patients. I watched as he popped the plant out of the pot and dug a hole in the soil. With careful fingers he loosened the roots and set the plant into the newly dug hole. He patted a mound of dirt around it and sprinkled it with water from a nearby copper watering can.

With a smile he said, "Now, she has everything she needs to live." He handed me a plant and observed me as I did the same thing. My plant rested in the soil next to his, but I still didn't get it. "Those two plants look exactly the same, don't they?"

"Yeah, I guess so." Was this a horticulture quiz? If he expected me to have any knowledge about plants or growing anything, he was sorely mistaken. I smiled, eager to carry on our conversation.

"They are very similar. They come from the same root stock, but the offshoots are noticeably different. If you look closely at those two garden boxes, you'll see the differences pretty clearly. For instance, this root stock produces red flowers, and those produce pink and white flowers. If you mix up the cuttings before you plant them, if you don't watch what you're doing, you'll have to take a chance on what you end up with. You can't be sure what you have until well after the planting, after the flowers begin to bloom." He watched me patiently.

"Avery, we Dufresnes, all of us, come from the same root stock, but there are offshoots that grow wild in our family tree. And these wild roots would destroy us, if we allowed them to grow for too long or too deeply."

"Doesn't every family tree have those, Mitchell? There's no way an old family like ours doesn't have secrets and 'wild offshoots.' What are you trying to tell me? Are we inbred? Do we have Yankee forefathers? Do we have a pirate lineage?" I laughed dryly, but apparently he didn't like my attempts at humor. "Please cut to the chase."

He didn't, though. He was committed to leading me to whatever understanding he hoped I would achieve. "These wild offshoots are pure stock, more like weeds. They aren't as hearty; they don't hold up to the heat. Did you know that weeds strangle flowers?"

I peeled off the gloves and tossed them in the box. "No, I can't say that I did know that."

"If you saw the videos, you know this already—the battle of the bloodlines continues, Avery. The wild offshoots are at it again. The conflict has never let up. You know about Athena and Susanna, Ambrose and Chase?"

"Yes, I know. So? Chase had two wives. Two cousins fought over Susanna—an unfortunate girl who had few prospects other than to marry a white man. That's the big story? That wasn't uncommon for the time. It's historical fact."

"No, that's not the big story." Mitchell peeled off his gloves too, his patience with me finally fading. "Which blood calls to you, Avery? Because the battle isn't just a bit of family history for you. It's a reality. The battle continues—the one that began almost two hundred years ago. The question now is which blood calls to you, Avery?"

"I don't get this at all. Are you talking about DNA? Blood types?"

"Well, in modern terms, yes. But I'm not sure that has anything to do with it, really. I think the blood differences are more subtle. Although Aunt Anne would disagree with me."

"Am I supposed to take a test? And if I did, what would that prove?"

"I don't know. That you have old blood? I'm going to tell you what I know, but that's not much. Not really."

"Please do. Because if I don't get answers soon, I'm getting in my car and heading north until I run out of gas. I can't deal with ghosts and the supernatural, and currently there is an abundance of both. There, I said it! I'm seeing ghosts and dreaming about them! Does that make me certifiable? Am I the wild offshoot you were talking about?" I sat down on a wooden bench, uncaring that I plopped down in a pile of dirt.

"Oh no, Avery. That's not what I meant. Aunt Anne always said I was horrible at explaining things. That's not what I meant." I couldn't help but cry. Mitchell sat beside me and let me lay my head on his shoulder until I got it together. In a whisper he said, "Tell me more about the spirits. What are you seeing?"

"There are spirits at Sugar Hill—and Thorn Hill. I've seen Ms. Roberts, and Susanna and even Ambrose. The portrait of Chase keeps changing, but he's always staring at me. Why? How am I expected to deal with this? What do they want, and how do I make it stop?"

He sighed sadly. "I wish I had an answer, for you and for Summer. I think she believes I plotted against her, but it wasn't like that. Poor Summer. My sister wanted to be the matrone so badly, but it could never be. She was instantly disqualified once Miss Anne knew whose blood ran strongest in her."

"Why would that matter? That seems very cruel. Summer would have been a good matrone."

His voice dropped down to a whisper, and he seemed very uncomfortable. "Hardly. She would have done the Lovely Man's bidding. It was inevitable. Up until now, the women in our family have managed to keep the spirit at bay, most of them. But the spirit's strength increases with every new matrone. And he...the one I spoke of...he wants his lost Susanna. He wants her and will never stop searching for her. Even in death he hasn't ceased his search."

"I don't believe any of it, Mitchell! Surely this is family legend. Just gossip—just rumors."

"Are you saying that you haven't had the dream? The dream of kissing Ambrose? Summer did. She bragged about it, she told Vertie. I heard her confess it." He shook his head in disgust and kept on, "The Lovely Man is what they call him when they don't want to say his name. If you say his name, and you belong to him, he is bound to come if you call, especially if you wear the ring."

"But I don't have his blood, from what you say. What if I did not dream about Ambrose? What if it was Chase I dreamed of? Or somebody else."

"Tell me exactly what you dreamed, Avery. Don't leave anything out."

I rubbed my dirty hands on my blue jeans. I could hardly believe I was going to tell him this, but I was. And why? Did I believe any of this? I wasn't sure yet, but I said I wanted answers.

Maybe it was finally time to hear the truth.

Chapter Fourteen – Avery

"It happened last night. The My Haunted Plantation crew encountered a problem during their investigation of the basement. One of the investigators, Jessica, claimed she saw two ghosts in the basement, including the ghost of Regina Dufresne. Jessica says Regina had been walled up in the basement. After the incident was over, she couldn't remember anything, but they have it all on film. Obviously we couldn't let them continue, so they are poking around other properties today. The Ramparts, I think. Right now, probably as we speak, Reed has his friend from the university searching for anomalies in the walls."

"I see," Mitchell said as he stood, dusting off his clothes.

"I decided not to return to Thorn Hill. I went to my bedroom at Sugar Hill, but something strange happened. Well, actually, the strangeness began before I arrived. I rode over from Thorn Hill with Jamie. You remember, Jamie, my detective friend? He was always so level-headed. Well, he began telling about this déjà vu he'd been having. How he thought he'd been here before, at Sugar Hill and Thorn Hill, how he could not remember parts of his childhood until he met me. He lived here, in Belle Fontaine. Can you believe that?"

"Surprising."

"Yes, and he wasn't himself. He pulled the car over and began telling me he loved me and that he had lived here before, that he knew me before." Mitchell's eyes widened at the details, but he kept quiet. I continued rambling on, trying to get it all out.

"We got the call about Jessica's paranormal episode and came back to Sugar Hill to see what happened. Later that night, Reed kissed me. Not just a friendly kiss. He kissed me! I went upstairs to my room and locked the door. I fell asleep and dreamed...dreamed about kissing him." I couldn't look Mitchell in the eyes. "But it wasn't him, it was Jamie. And if that's not bad enough, then I was kissing Ambrose, and then Chase."

"Go on." Mitchell's facial expression did not reveal what he thought about me. "Keep going, Avery."

"I think...I think I was Susanna because it was Chase I wanted, Chase I wanted with all my heart and soul. I saw her. She told me that there was no escape from Ambrose, that he was my soul mate. What kind of nightmare was that?"

"Not a nightmare, Avery. You were there."

"Well, to make matters worse, I woke up with Jamie in my bed. He was sleeping, and we were both naked. I am pretty sure we had sex, but it must have been during the dream. I don't know what to make of all this. I am so freaked out that I don't know what to do!" This would have been a good place to start crying again, but I didn't. I was too wound up from uncovering the truth.

"Don't beat yourself up over it. It was bound to happen sooner or later. It always does."

"What does it mean, Mitchell?"

"You have to finish the videos, Avery. Don't let the supernatural activity distract you. Keep watching. You'll find out what you want to know. Ask Reed about Vertie's journals. Demand that he give them to you—today. Then lock yourself away and watch and read until you know it all. Only then will you fully understand what is at stake here."

"You can't just tell me? Don't pretend you don't know what's happening around the house."

"There is a war going on, Avery. It was going on long before you got here, and unless you can end it, it will go on after you have gone. It must come to an end. At last. Aunt Anne wanted to be the one to finish it, but she wasn't strong enough. But you can. You are strong, Avery. You *can* do it."

Excited that I was beginning to understand at least a little bit, I said, "Tell me more about the war, Mitchell. How do I win it? Who is fighting it?"

"It is for the soul of the family, the soul of the matrone. That ring you wear is the symbol of a promise made long ago. A promise to love and cherish, in sickness and in health, but that promise was cursed and a new spell was cast upon that ring. The spell bound the wearer to her soul mate for all eternity."

"So what belonged to Chase now belongs to Ambrose? Because of this ring?"

"It's more complicated than that, I think, Avery."

"I don't know if I believe this about a soul mate. I thought that was a phrase teenagers used."

"Oh, it's more than a phrase." His voice sank even lower. I could barely hear him now. "Soul mates aren't always star-crossed lovers. What if your soul mate was, in this current lifetime, someone you were repulsed by? What then? Would you still want to be bound to him?"

"Am I bound to some soul mate that I don't know? How can that be? Help me get this thing off!" I tugged at the ring desperately.

"You can't. It won't let you. Others have tried."

"Tell me who it is I am bound to, Mitchell. Is it Ambrose or Chase? Or someone else?"

I heard footsteps in the leaves outside the hothouse. Apparently so did Mitchell. He froze and looked at the door. Whoever it was didn't come in.

In a whisper he said, "That's for you to figure out, Avery. You could turn your back on it all, like Aunt Anne did for a time. She married a man she loved, had children. But in the end, the call home was too great, and she came back to Belle Fontaine and into the arms of danger. Her husband died only a month later. Then her two daughters were found drowned. It was a terrible time for everyone."

"You are too young to remember that, I am sure."

"Not as young as I once was." He smiled wryly.

"Why me?"

He didn't answer but squeezed my hand quickly. He stared at the door again, but still no one entered.

I decided it was time to go. I'd put him in an awkward position already. Now we were being spied upon. I couldn't stay here in the hothouse all day. I had to retrieve Vertie's journals. I had to know what her thoughts were on the matter. I needed to hear her in order to know how to move forward.

"Thank you, Mitchell. I hope that someday you will take me up on that offer and come spend some time with me at Sugar Hill."

He smiled and murmured goodbye. I flung open the hothouse door to bust whoever was hanging around out there, but I saw nothing. No stirring of the leaves, not a living soul. I glanced over my shoulder, but Mitchell was already sliding his gloves back on. I walked back to the house by myself. Feeling determined to get to the bottom of the family mysteries, I grabbed my keys off the side table and walked to the front door. I closed the cottage door behind me and got in my car.

I didn't have to wonder where to go next. I headed straight for D & D, where I knew Reed would be. No sense in waiting until later.

If Mitchell couldn't tell me the truth, I'd have to find it out myself. After all, I had once been America's Newscaster.

If I couldn't uncover the meaning of all this, who could?

Chapter Fifteen – Jessica

I felt fine today. I had my energy back and was excited about exploring the woods near the Ramparts. Imagine, someone burned the settlement down to the ground and they'd never rebuilt the place. But then again, why would you want to rebuild on cursed land? I shivered at the thought.

Honestly, I had no idea if this land was cursed or not, and I decided right then and there I would keep a level head. No guesses. I tapped my lip with my finger as I flipped through the photos I'd taken of interesting spots in the woods.

But if I were to go with my feelings on this place, I'd have to say it *felt* cursed. The dead grass and the acidic-looking sandy soil were proof that nothing grew here. Nothing at all. According to Megan's research, over a hundred people died the night the Ramparts burned down. Many were slaves who'd been confined to what essentially were jail cells. Those unfortunate souls didn't stand a chance when the fire swept through the dry wooden buildings, and they weren't the first slated for rescue. The fire moved quickly, spreading so fast that no number of buckets of water would have made a difference, even if the slaves had been accorded some compassion.

Shanty houses and larger residences along the main avenue burned to the ground first. There was no specific list of names, but we easily found enough evidence to know that this terrible tragedy really had occurred. There were supposedly two cemeteries nearby that attested to that fact. Thankfully for us, Reed Dufresne wasn't arguing this point. We found pieces of charred wood, stone foundations and the odd artifact here and there, including some old buttons and broken glass. I held them in the hopes that I would experience some kind of energy, but I felt nothing.

We did some tests in the woods, checking for blips in the electromagnetic field, and tried to get a baseline reading, but there wasn't anything noticeable to report. Still, we recorded our findings, as we always did.

Becker suggested voice testing, and of course we picked up nothing. It was pretty darn discouraging, but in true boss-man fashion Mike had a plan for tonight's follow-up investigation.

After lunch we settled on three areas to monitor with our cameras. We set up an IR camera at the old town well, another in the ruins of a burned-out home and two more near some twisted oak trees that looked to be several hundred years old. They were near an interesting rock formation, and I felt there might be something there, but the machines registered zero.

We went back inside the van; it was just the four of us now, Mike, Becker, Megan and me. James and the new camera guy were sleeping in James' truck. At least I didn't have to listen to James snore. That man sounded like a mucus-filled freight train.

There were no cameras rolling in the van, but we did our job anyway. As Mike pointed out once, "We belong to the network, guys. You never know when they'll hit the record button on any of these machines." I glanced around the van, as if I could detect any hidden devices. I wouldn't really know what I was looking for if I saw it. Until my work with My Haunted Plantation, my most sophisticated ghost hunting device was a handheld tape recorder.

"Okay, Camera One. Let's light you up," Becker said to the camera and watched as the picture came in clearly now.

"Camera One online," I reported even though I sat next to him. Soon everything was working properly and all the cameras passed our initial tests.

Mike said with a forced yawn, "All right, let's get some sleep, guys. Thankfully, we've got the two vans, and there's plenty of room for anyone who wants to catch some sleep if you can. No time to go back to the hotel. That goes for you too, Megan. You'll have to stay. I appreciate all your research efforts, but I need you fresh for this investigation tonight. We'll work together tonight; Becker and Jess will take the second shift."

"You think we'll catch something out here, or is this just to keep us safely away from the house? I'm dying to get back in that old plantation. You know, I meant to mention this earlier while we were rolling, but I had the strangest dream about that place last night."

Megan tapped her plump, glossed lips with her manicured finger. She had bright blond hair, a fake tan, fake nails and fake eyelashes. And she was gorgeous. I was a no-muss, no-fuss kind of gal, and the differences between us were apparent. Guys preferred Megan. I was okay with that, but the network? Not so much. I had a feeling that part of my negotiations for next season would involve enhancements to my looks. I was not going to go to the lengths Megan did. Breast implants were not in my future, and I refused to color my hair. But then again, I wasn't sure I'd be staying on anyway.

"You too? I thought it was just me. I was standing on the very top of the house, like in the crow's nest, and I saw in the distance a big ship coming in…"

"Hey, I don't interrupt your stories, Beck," Megan growled at him.

"Enough with the stories, guys. Let's hit the hay for a bit. It's getting cold out." Mike shoved his hands in his jacket pockets and glanced up at the sky. "At least it's going to be a dry night."

I noticed that Mike and Megan left the van tentatively holding hands. That settled it. I'd sleep in the media van, even if that meant obsessively staring at the cameras and listening for erratic beeps from the charging REM pods. We wouldn't deploy them until right before we headed out in a few hours. It would be completely black out soon. I wondered if we'd have any moon tonight. Hmm...I'd have to check that online.

"I'm out, Jess. Going to sleep in the truck with James and Victor, I guess. You want to come with, cuddle with me?"

"What would your Dufresne friend think about that?"

"Who cares? She's about as serious as I am."

I waved my hand dismissively but couldn't help but grin at his honesty. "That's gross, Becker. You shouldn't just sleep with anyone and everyone."

"I don't and you know it. Now I ask you again, pretty lady. You want to cuddle?"

"I don't know..." I said sweetly, "are you the last man on earth?" I propped my legs up in his empty chair.

"No, but this might be your last chance," he shot back playfully.

"No thanks, I'll die a virgin. Good night, Becker!"

"Oh my God! You're a virgin? I can't tell you how that turns me on." He hopped back in the van and stood very close to me now, smiling down flirtatiously, "I can help you with that, Jess."

"Gross. Get out of here and close the door behind you." I stuck my tongue out at him, and he responded with a blown kiss as he departed. I wasn't that offended. Jeffrey Becker had only one speed—fast forward—and it was hard for me to take any guy who wore a messy man-bun seriously. However, if he took that long hair down, it might be another story. I had a weakness for long-haired guys. Well, if he weren't such a floozy. Nope. Absolutely not interested in Jeffrey Becker and his amazingly uninhibited sexuality.

Before he closed the door he said in a totally adult and concerned voice, "Be careful out there tonight, Jess."

Wrapping my jacket around my shoulders tighter, I smiled bleakly. "You got it." He closed the door, and I wrapped my arms around my knees and turned my attention to the cameras. All four were working fine and were live-streaming the images. We hadn't hit record on any of them yet; we couldn't afford to waste all that data, and who the heck wanted to scan through an extra four hours of video? Not me. And with Megan back in her position as the queen of MHP, Mike giving interviews and Beck fixing something, all the grunt work would fall to me. I was like an intern, but at least I was a well-paid intern.

I forgot all about checking on the moonrise, and soon I felt sleepy. Staring at four boring feeds was bound to put me to sleep. What was I thinking? I pulled the chair closer and propped my legs up again. That did it. I was totally comfortable now and soon fell asleep.

I didn't dream a thing, which felt like pure bliss. Memories of the past pushed at the edges of my dream, but thankfully tragedy didn't infringe on my slumber.

But a weird sound did.

It sounded as if something caught on fire and exploded, like a gas bomb. The whole dang van shook! It reminded me of when my dad would get carried away with the charcoal grill. He'd soak the thing with lighter fluid and then toss in a match. Yes, it sounded just like that. I woke up feeling stiff but didn't waste any time tightening in on Camera Three's screen. Becker had marked it with tape and paper: BURNED-OUT HOUSE. Then the light disappeared.

"Okay, I'm seeing things." I rubbed my eyes and moved the camera around again to get a better view. Then I heard the sound again and saw the flash of light. That was definitely a ball of heat rising from the ground, but where did it come from? I zoomed in, but there was a significant amount of foliage in the way. A fleeting dark figure shot across the screen and disappeared before I could hit record. I had the camera recording everything now. *Heck, I might as well turn them all on!* And I did.

As I waited, I thought about the sound and what I saw. It seemed as if the sound and the flash of light went together, but how could they? The audio icon plainly displayed what I already knew. The red toggle overlaid the speaker—the sound had not been turned on yet. It would have been impossible to hear the audio before now.

Which led me to just one conclusion...I wasn't hearing these things in the natural world. The burning sounds were a residual haunt. That was hopeful! Barring a gas leak or some other kind of real-world explanation, this was proof of supernatural activity. These were echoes from the spiritual world, and because of my psychic receptivity I could hear them. I reached for the walkie-talkie, and my finger hovered over the button. I'd jumped the gun before, made a fool of myself in the basement of Sugar Hill. I couldn't even remember the event! Not with any clarity. Was I really going to jeopardize my spot on the show by "crying wolf" again?

Hell no. My heart pounded as I watched the flash of light appear again in front of Camera Three. *I wonder what would happen if I took the IR filter off the camera.* With nervous fingers I tapped on the keyboard, just like I'd seen Becker do a hundred times. *Ha! Look at that! I'm a technician now too. Take that, my playboy friend.*

I'd have to do this investigation by myself. I grabbed the recorder, a camera and the walkie and headed out of the van to the ruins of the burned-out building. It was as dark as a bottomless pit out tonight. Even the stars disapproved of my idea because they didn't appear at all. No moon either. No need to Google that now.

I slid the items on my belt and zipped my jacket. Thankfully, I had a fleece hat stuffed in one of my pockets, a navy blue one that my mother had sent me last month. It was kind of ratty, obviously not new, but I was grateful. I didn't mind her penny-pinching ways. She'd been a good mother to me.

I suddenly missed home. I missed them all. But here I was, searching for proof of the paranormal. In the dark. In the woods. In Alabama. Absently I wondered what my mother told her nosy friends about me.

"Oh, you know, Jessica has always been a bit of a free spirit. Always one to peek behind the curtain. I'm so proud of my special girl."

Special girl as in, *"God? Why did you send me this weird child, and what do I do with her now that I have her?"* Yes, I could imagine her saying just that.

I glanced behind me and didn't see anyone looking. The camera truck lights didn't come on, and the van lights were off. Mike and Megan were probably fast asleep or doing something I didn't want to know about.

I decided to do it. I hadn't quite made up my mind until I got there. But now that I hovered at the edge of the forest, I was definitely going to do it.

As I took a step inside the foliage I heard a sound behind me.

"Jessica! What the hell are you doing?"

"Jesus, Becker! You scared the hell out of me." I laughed and squatted in the grass trying to catch my breath. "Keep your voice down. Something is moving on Camera Three, and I'm going to check it out. It's probably nothing. You stay here." I waved him back and rose.

"Hell no, I'm not letting you investigate without me. Mike never gives me a break. I want to go with you."

"I don't think..."

"You let me come along, or I go wake up Mike and Megan in the shaggin' wagon. And the camera crews."

I sighed and shrugged. "Fine, but I'm taking the lead."

He ran beside me as we jogged down the path. "Stop right here," I said. "Let's take some readings. The house is just over there. That's where we need to be."

Before we had a chance to do any sweeps or take any pictures, we saw a fire. A big roaring fire, like someone wanted to have a bonfire tonight, right out here in the woods. It burst up from the ground like something that had always been there.

"What the hell? Who did this?" Naturally, Becker ran toward the fire without looking first. I knew what he was thinking, *somebody lit this fire, and I'm going to find out who it was!* It was a good thought, but I knew the truth. The person who set this fire had been dead a long time.

How did I know this?

Because I could see her. I could see her eyes, and they were full of hatred.

And they were staring at me.

Chapter Sixteen – Avery

Naturally, Reed wasn't anywhere to be found at D & D. The sweet receptionist smiled but didn't provide me with any additional information. I mused over waiting for him, but I got the feeling he didn't want to see me. Well, if he wasn't here, then he must be at Sugar Hill. That's where I headed next. It was time to have it out—over a few things. Like how dare he kiss me without my permission! And how dare he hold back vital information from me.

I found him easily enough, sitting in the back of a truck talking to a man I didn't recognize. I could see an ambulance leaving as I pulled up. That could mean one of two things. Either they found a body— or two—or they found nothing. By the look on Reed's handsome face, I could tell which one it was.

He shook his friend's hand and they said their good-byes as I got out of my Lexus. I wanted to punch him in the face. That all changed when I saw he'd been crying.

"What is it, Reed? What happened?" I touched him discreetly on the shoulder. As always he was the picture of Southern perfection with his perfectly starched shirt and creased trousers.

He rubbed his eyes quickly, like he had never intended to let me see him crying. Maybe he wouldn't have, but I didn't give him a chance to hide.

"They found the bodies, just like Jessica said. I can hardly believe it. How can she know that, Avery? Now the police want to talk to her. They think she has something to do with this."

I couldn't help but laugh. "They think Jessica played some role in a two-hundred-year-old murder case? What is she? A time traveler? Sounds like the local police department has a problem with logic," I said dryly.

"If you want to know the truth, it's not Jessica Chesterfield they suspect. It's us. They think the Dufresnes are pulling a family stunt. They think we knew about this and wanted to put it all on television. Or *you* wanted to put it on television. They have this idea that you're using it as your big break back into News Quarter."

"Do what? They think I wanted to find our dead ancestors buried in a wall? Why would I need to pull a publicity stunt? I'm doing everything I can to stay out of the press, not invite them here." I sat on the bumper of his vehicle with my arms crossed.

"Well, that's not how they see it, and you can't blame them."

"How is that, Reed?"

"Well, they only know you as America's Newscaster, the woman who went after Senator Greeley and humiliated him in front of the nation. They don't believe you have any qualms about playing this family secret to your advantage."

"That's just great." Once again that interview came back to haunt me. For the first time I truly felt regret over it.

"As far as the bodies go, the initial examination shows that one was a young female and the other was likely an older female. There were only fragments of their clothing left, but they were wearing jewelry that might belong to the Dufresne collection. But that's not the most disturbing thing."

"Really? Well, do tell. As if that wasn't disturbing enough." Yeah, I felt like being a smart-ass today. After he gave Jessica such a hard time, it was good to see Reed eating some crow. He was too damn cocky, I'd decided on my way over here. Could a matrone fire the family attorney?

"My friend Greg said the inside of the wall definitely had scratch marks, just like you would find if someone were walled in. They died in there. They were trapped—buried alive. This is horrible! What if the My Haunted Plantation people or the Paranormal Channel get a hold of this? They are going to have a field day! We don't need our dirty laundry aired in public, Avery. We need to come up with a plan. Damn Aunt Anne for this! How could she have brought them here? She had to be out of her flipping mind! Now people will be asking all sorts of questions."

"Who cares? Let them question us. What do we have to hide now? I don't think it can get any worse than skeletons in the basement, can it?"

He gave me a look that suggested I was wrong. I didn't probe him further. "Obviously Aunt Anne knew what they would find, and you don't have to clean up anything, Reed. I'll do it."

He ran his hands through his dark hair. "What? What do you mean?"

"I mean, I can handle this. I'm America's Newscaster! As you pointed out. I think I can handle a few bodies buried in the ancestral home. It's not earth-shaking news, Reed. You act like it is the end of the world. I think the best thing to do is put our cards on the table. Be honest. Tell the investigators the truth! Say, 'We know we have family secrets. Help us uncover them!' If you do that, you control the information. If you don't, they'll report what they want."

"We can't do that!"

"It's done." I stepped closer to him. "Aunt Anne named me matrone for a reason. She must have known what she was doing, that they would find those bodies and whatever else this family has hidden. It's time to shine some light into the past, Reed. I want to use these investigators. I want answers, damn it!"

"Avery, I don't think you know what that means. This could be bad for us."

"How? How can it be bad? Explain it to me, and please stop being so cryptic!"

"There are certain factions that want to see you fail. They think we need another matrone to lead us."

That felt like a slap in the face. "Who do they have in mind, then? Pepper?"

"No. They want Summer. I guess there is no sense in hiding that from you now."

"I see. And is that how you feel, Reed? Do you want Summer to take my place?"

"No, I don't want that. Aunt Anne picked you, but I'm only one person. And I can't help you if you don't listen to me."

Blinking back angry tears I said, "This is how we are going to do things, and they can like it or they can lump it! I don't need the board's permission to handle this. I'm not asking for their permission—or their money. I have money of my own. It's time to put these ghosts to rest. And not just for me, but for you too, Reed. For you, our families, and our children."

"I don't even have a girlfriend. Having children seems a long way off, but I see what you mean." He smiled for the first time in a while. "Very well, let's do it your way, Avery. Let's embrace this and see what happens. You're right, of course; if we want to control the information we need to come at it differently, try a new tack. Yes, let's do that."

"Fine. Now where are my Grandmother Vertie's journals, Reed? I think it's pretty crappy of you to hide them from me. You know I need to read them!"

"I did no such thing. I left them here with Robin. She said she would deliver them to you."

"She did not. You should never have released those to anyone but me, Reed. I can't believe you."

"Oh, I'm sorry. I didn't think it was a big deal. She seemed so devoted to you; I just assumed that she would do what she said."

"I've got to go, Reed. I've got some studying to do before I see the My Haunted Plantation people tomorrow. Can you tell them I want to see them in the afternoon? I should be ready by then."

"What are you going to tell them?"

"Surely we can have them help us solve some minor family mysteries. Like what's the deal with this ring? How do we get rid of the ghosts here and at Thorn Hill?"

He nodded, and his handsome face softened. "About the other night..."

"Must we discuss this now?" I said without a smile on my face. "To tell you the truth, I have a few other things on my mind." I lied to his face and didn't let on how I really felt. *Of course, I've thought about that kiss and the ones that followed in my dreams. Who are you, Reed Dufresne?* I turned and walked into the house, leaving him standing in the driveway.

I called out for Robin a few times. She never came, so I jogged up my stairs and called her from my room intercom. "Robin, can you tell me where those journals are? The ones Reed sent over from Aunt Vertie?"

"The green ones?" she called back, sounding like she was a million miles away. Something was wrong with the call box. I banged on it but lost her. Had that even been Robin's voice?

Then a tap on my door came. I opened it, and to my surprise there was a cardboard box with a stack of green journals peeking out the top. How the heck did they get up here that fast? I caught a whiff of familiar perfume. Yes, I knew that smell. That was Edith Roberts!

I grabbed the box, slammed the door and stepped away from it. My heart was pounding in my chest. I heard the light tapping on the door and nearly jumped out of my skin. "Who is it?"

"It's Robin! Sorry to bother you."

With a sigh of relief, I opened the door. "No bother at all. I'm just glad you're alive."

Her face paled and she said, "I'm sorry about the intercom. It's behaving badly today. What did you need? Those journals? I set them on the table downstairs, but when I went back to get them they were missing. I assumed you had picked them up, but I guess you didn't?" She looked embarrassed, and then her face lit up. "Oh good! You found them! Thank the Lord! Anything else?"

"No...I think that's...that's all for now, Robin. I would like to be alone this morning. I don't want any calls or visitors for the next few hours."

"Okay, well, let me know if I can help you with anything. Call me if you need me. What about supper?"

"I'll sneak down for something later." I closed the door behind her and picked up the box. I put it on the coffee table and flipped on the television and VCR. Might as well do the whole thing. As a news anchor, I learned to take in information in strange ways. For example, I could listen to two news shows simultaneously, read three magazines *and* listen to talk radio. And I retained all that information. I had this weird ability to scan and process large amounts of information with just my mind and could retain most of it. I would put that skill to work for me tonight. I was going to watch the videos and read the books. I felt such an urgency to get this done. I had to! It was almost as if a life hung in the balance.

Maybe more than my own.

Chapter Seventeen – Susanna Serene

I was sitting at the desk in the study when Ambrose began calling for me. I didn't hurry to respond to him. I had one or two more numbers to record, and then I would close the books for tonight. The oil lamp flickered on my desk and a wind threatened to blow up a storm outside. But I'd heard the carriage come around and knew that my husband's cousin would be leaving soon. I supposed he wanted to say goodbye, perhaps attempt to make me jealous. I could have told him he was wasting his time. Since my return to Thorn Hill, my heart had been empty of love. Love was a betrayer, not a thing to be trusted. It always led you astray, and I refused to be betrayed by it any longer.

Business continued to grow, and thanks to a few unique acquisitions this month I had no shortage of customers. The blue print fabric with the gold leaves was an exceptional find. I smiled at the memory of the recent bidding war that bolt of fabric had caused. Everyone was still talking about it. In the end, Evelyn LaGrange won the prize, ensuring that her daughter would be the one to wear it. She and no other. Silly women.

What a strange few years it had been! I always expected to become a mother and a happy wife, but in the end I had achieved neither of those girlhood dreams. At least I had this.

I was an independent woman now. Or as independent as the law would allow me to be. I had a business of my own, a legitimate business, and who did I have to thank for that? Ambrose. Despite his threats to me the night he rescued me from the Ramparts, he had not punished me. But I kept my end of the bargain. I never mentioned his cousin's name, and I never again asked to see Chase.

Once had been enough.

The man I loved was gone. In his place was a black-hearted plantation owner and his beastly little plain-faced wife. She'd never darkened my doors, but many of her friends had—and the stories they told! There were no happy times at Sugar Hill, apparently. I did not pry, and many times I changed the subject pretending I knew nothing about Chase or his wife Athena. It was better to feign ignorance than become embroiled in gossip. The fear he would divorce and disown me did not loom over me as it once had. I was established; I had a name for myself. I was no castoff anymore.

Good riddance! If Chase divorced me, as the rumor mill reported he eventually would, so much the better. I could marry Ambrose or someone else to keep my freedom, if pressed to do so. I had no shortage of kind eyes upon me.

Oddly enough, thanks to Ambrose's generosity, I had everything I needed. I had cornered the market here. If you wanted fine silk, you had to see me. Or at least visit my shop in the Ramparts. I alone determined who purchased those fine fabrics, and even the proper white women had to come to me to get the most beautiful prints! Oh, how it burned their hearts to do so! It was always a humorous sight to see their fine carriages roll up in front of my store.

Yes, the rumors still flew.

I was a left-hand wife, an adulteress in some people's eyes, and even to this day I was living like a whore with my lover. They said all these things, sometimes to my face. But they couldn't help themselves. Despite their disgust for me, they came with coins in hand, behaved as politely as they could during our business exchanges and left with the fabric they wanted. On a few occasions I had even refused to sell silk. It was my prerogative. Ambrose rarely came to the shop, but when he did it was to deliver some good news about a new supplier or a potential customer.

Ambrose and I were wealthy. Very wealthy indeed. So wealthy that even Etienne could not touch me anymore. I could buy her and sell her if I chose to. From all accounts she was very sick. And I wished her nothing but death. Just as she had delivered to my daughter. Somehow she had caused my daughter's death. I knew it in my bones. Despite my requests for information, my offers of money, she told me nothing.

Rarely did a man darken my shop door. Oh no, these fine women would never allow their husbands to visit me. I laughed at their disdain. I reviewed the numbers once more and smiled approvingly at this month's revenues.

I hated to admit it, but Ambrose was something of a genius when it came to business. He knew everyone, even though most wouldn't admit to that. In a way, he was like me.

A castoff, an unmentionable.

Recently he had secretly moved against the Mobile businesses, singlehandedly destroying their silk trade market with a few well-placed fires. Of course, he never admitted to such behavior, unless I plied him with liquor. And even then he did not share details. Ambrose was no fool. He knew better than to trust anyone.

Especially me. He felt the fire that burned in me. He knew that beneath my sweet smile and polite words I wanted nothing more than to drive a knife through his heart.

And so it was very smart of him to keep quiet. I hated him with a passion so deep it drove me to fantasize about killing him. To his face I smiled sweetly, kissed him often and did all that he asked when the lights went out, but secretly I seethed inside. His betrayal and abandonment would never be erased, no matter what good deeds he did on my behalf now. My heart and my pride demanded punishment—for them both! Both he and Chase should pay for what they had wrought in my life. My daughter was gone, and no amount of money or status could replace her—or the life I had intended for her.

Those first few months, how many times did I walked the halls of Thorn Hill in a dreamlike state, looking for her? Ambrose would find me and lead me back to bed, my tears flowing. But that did not happen anymore. I gave up my nighttime searches. I gave up the tears. I had no tears left anymore. Afterwards I walked the halls remembering the curses Sulli taught me. I cast them about like invisible nets over everything. Over every fine statue, every painting, every rug. I covered the place with my hate until I had nothing left.

Sometimes, after nights with Ambrose, I imagined I loved him. But when the sun rose, I remembered the pain of yesterday and hated him all over again.

Ambrose the beautiful. Ambrose the clever. Ambrose the vain. The thief of my happiness! The murderer of my soul!

Sometimes I let my guard down and allowed myself to feel the hatred fully, to revel in it. In those moments, he would look up from his book or his letters. It was as if he sensed my white-hot hate, for he would remind me of my tie to him. "Tell me, my soul mate. What are you thinking?" I would make something up, talk about business or the latest silk shipment, and he would ask no more questions. He knew something was amiss but felt satisfied not to push me.

Tired of waiting for me now, Ambrose appeared in the doorway. "Come see me off, my love. Or won't you miss me at all?"

"Of course I shall miss you. Who will I have to talk to while you're gone?"

"I know you, you'll keep busy. You work too hard, Susanna Serene. You should enjoy the fruits of your labor." He leaned against the doorway, his hat in his hands. He wore his hair loose tonight; the dark locks looked even darker against his white shirt. As always his full lips were bright red, and he had some extra color in his cheeks, proof that he'd enjoyed a few sips of his favorite brandy not long ago. Ambrose was tall and slender with a regal bearing that made him appear even taller. He had a handsome face, and if I didn't know the truth about his black heart, I might love him.

I slid my arm through his and walked him to the door. He continued, "I'll only be gone for a few weeks, my dear. In the meantime, don't work yourself to death. Do remember to come home and rest at night, Susanna. You look thin. Maybe you should visit the shop less. Let Ingrid handle the customers for a few days."

"Oh, how can I do that? Mrs. Daugherty and Mrs. Forsythe are coming tomorrow. Ingrid would give them the store if I left her alone. You know she doesn't have the mind for negotiations."

He took my face in his hands and kissed me. Despite my hatred for him, desire grew within me, and I knew he knew that. He smiled down at me through slitted eyes. "You do what you think is right. I'll be home soon." I didn't ask him where he was going or what he was doing. I didn't have to ask. I knew. These visits started at the beginning of spring. Ambrose had left the house and gone to the Ramparts; he said he was going to see a man there. But the truth was he had a girl there, a younger girl, Ingrid told me.

"Her name is Coquette. Mr. Ambrose messes with her. You want me to fix her?"

Of course, I had no desire to do such a thing. It was no bother to me; if he was with her, he wasn't with me and I did not have to pretend to feel affection for him. In fact, it helped me to remember how much I hated him. My heart was a deceitful thing that I could never depend on.

I watched the carriage roll away but didn't wave or make any friendly gesture, even when he waved to me.

It was the day before Easter, and I decided to retire early. Mass was at sunrise, and I planned to attend. I needed all the peace I could gather to keep my soul from lighting on fire. I ate a simple meal: a piece of bread and a slice of salted ham. As I slipped into my tub, I watched the lightning flash across the water.

A storm had rolled in off the Mobile Bay, and from my second-floor vantage point I could see the ships lolling on the waters. I prayed that my fabrics had been safely unloaded without damage. When my bathwater became chilly, I slipped out and dried myself off; I'd sent my servants to bed. I had no slaves—I detested the practice and insisted that Ambrose not have them either.

I wrapped my blue gown around me and tied the ribbon at my neck. Then I heard the sound. Someone was knocking at the door downstairs. I took the candle beside me and headed down to see who would call on me at such an hour. To my surprise, the door opened, seemingly on its own, and I stood watching and waiting for whomever or whatever it was to come in from the rain.

"Ambrose?"

It was not Ambrose. The man began to cough and sputter as if he had just been pulled out of the Mobile Bay. Then he fell in a heap on the ground. I waved the light over him and immediately recognized my visitor.

Chase!

I did not come to his rescue. Instead, I stood over him, unwilling to even lift him from the floor.

My housekeeper Nicole ran into the room, her gown half open. "I thought I heard—Miss Susanna! Who is that? Oh my word! It is a gentleman by his clothes! Did he say anything? What happened?"

Nicole wanted details, but I had nothing to tell her. "Call the doctor. Have John take him to the doctor. He doesn't belong here."

"Miss! You can't take him back out in the rain! Look at him! He's very near death, I think. He's not even awake!" She reached down and touched his forehead. "This man is burning up. We've got to get him to a couch or a bed. Somewhere warm."

"No!" I set the candle down. My hands were shaking too much to hold it. "He's not staying here! Put him outside and get John. Tell him to take him to Sugar Hill. They'll know what to do with him."

"Oh my Lord! Is this Chase Dufresne?"

"Do it, Nicole, or you can go too." I said quietly, evenly. I had never been anything but friendly to her before. "Take him away and mention nothing to anyone about his being here. Especially Ambrose."

"Very well, miss. But I hope you know you are sending him to his death." She made the sign of the cross as if it would protect her from anything that happened to him.

"I understand. Do as I ask." My heart bounced in my chest like a rabbit. What did this mean? As I began to climb the stairs, Chase began to call me.

"Susanna! Please, Susanna..."

I froze knowing that if I turned around, if I helped him, it might melt my heart. No, it wouldn't. I couldn't allow that, but I couldn't allow him to die either, could I? What would Ambrose say? What would he do if he were here? We never spoke of Chase, and I had no idea of his feelings for his cousin. Not truly.

"Please..."

His voice found it. The one small portion of me that cared whether he lived or died. I didn't want to be with him, and I didn't want to care about him, but I also did not want him to die. I walked down the stairs and called after Nicole, "Let's get him to the couch. Stoke the fire and ask John to fetch the doctor."

"Look, miss! He's bleeding! He's been shot or something!"

I fell on my knees beside him and pulled back his clothing. Yes, he had been shot. Gut shot. If he lived it would be a miracle. "Give me your gown!" Obediently Nicole stripped herself naked, and I used the garment to staunch the bleeding. "Get dressed and tell John to go find the doctor!" She scurried out of the room, and I sat on the cold floor with my dying husband.

"Susanna, forgive me," he whispered. His blue eyes were full of pain, and his blond hair was wet and sticky with mud. He must have fallen down a few times before he arrived at Thorn Hill. I lifted his head and put it in my lap, keeping one hand on the night-gown. Thankfully, the bleeding was slowing. Or so I hoped.

"Hush now, Chase. Don't talk. Keep still."

"I have wronged you. Forgive..." His words faded as he passed out, but his intention was clear. He wanted forgiveness. He wanted my forgiveness. This I had not expected. I had not dreamed this would happen.

Then the tears came. They slid down my face like two rivers. By the time the doctor arrived, Chase was barely breathing but still alive.

But for how long, and what would happen if Ambrose knew he were here? I couldn't think about that now. I had to think of Chase. He had to live!

No matter what it cost me.

Chapter Eighteen – Handsome Cheever

"Toting water up a hill with a bucket that's got a hole in it—that's what this is, Miss Billie. That's exactly what this is. But I got to go. You know Handsome has to go now, but I'll be back, Miss Billie." He packed the items in his bag and stepped outside his old wooden house. He did not have a fine home, nothing like Sugar Hill or the Rose Cottage, but it was his own place. And there were no ghosts there, only his angel, Miss Billie Holiday, who sang to him when trouble stirred up around him. It was stirring now for sure!

Ooh, what a little
Moonlight can do.

Ooh, what a little moonlight
Can do to you.

"I know, lady, but I don't have no choice. There's no moonlight, but I can't stay. Don't be mad at Handsome, Miss Billie. I have to go. I promised her I would. You know I have to."

You're in love.
Your heart's a-fluttering
All day long.

"Now, don't say that, Lady. I'm not in love with no one but you."

Handsome's son came out to see what he was doing, but Handsome had long given up trying to explain to him what he saw, what he heard. Lucas didn't understand that Handsome had an angel who sang to him when trouble drew near. And even though there was trouble lingering nearby, he was happy to hear her again. She never let him down. She wouldn't start now, surely.

He slid into the leather seat, waved at his son and backed the black Cadillac down the driveway. Handsome did not look back. It didn't matter that Lucas wouldn't approve of his mission. He didn't care.

He sang the song, right along with Miss Billie.

He was so grateful to have the use of this car. It was an older Cadillac, but it looked and smelled like new. Oh yes, Handsome liked to keep everything clean and tidy. He didn't have any other car; this car belonged to the Dufresnes, but it was like it was his. He couldn't drive around with a dirty car—that would not be caring for it properly. Only he rarely drove it anymore. Miss Avery never called his house. She didn't call and say, "Hey, Handsome! Bring that car up here!" Not like Miss Anne or Miss Margaret did. He usually got to run errands for the old matrone, but no more. He hardly had anything to do. But tonight—tonight she would need him.

Handsome made the sign of the cross as he eased out onto Jackson Lane. Miss Billie Holiday was singing a different song now, and he didn't take that as a good omen. He believed this was her favorite song.

All of me.
Why not take all of me?

Can't you see
I'm no good without you?

"No, no, Miss Billie. You won't be without me. I'm here! Handsome is listening!" He said nothing else, only hummed along to the music that played in his head. Her voice warned him sweetly but persistently.

Take my lips;
I want to lose them.

Take my arms;
I'll never use them.

Your goodbye
Left me with eyes that cry.
How can I go on, dear, without you?

You took the part
That once was my heart.
So why not take all of me...

He turned down the road that would lead to the outskirts of the Ramparts, for that was where he was going. He knew that, just as clearly as he heard Miss Billie's song in his ears and his heart. He patted the bag beside him. He hoped his collection of hoodoo talismans would help him, would protect him and help him save the lady. Just as his family had done for generations. Yes, he could do this. Sulli's blood ran through his veins. Strong blood, courageous blood.

I'm going! I'll give my life if you ask, but don't take my Miss Billie away! I love you, Miss Billie!

He could see the fire from the road. It was blazing, and it lit up the dark woods, sending the shadows scurrying for cover. Those weren't just any shadows, but dead things that wore shadows like cloaks.

Your goodbye
Left me with eyes that cry.
How can I go on, dear, without you?

You took the best,
So why not take the rest?

Baby, take all of me.

He hummed as he pulled the car off the road and grabbed his bag. He had a fire extinguisher in his trunk, but he knew it wouldn't do him any good. That wasn't any normal fire but a supernatural hoo-doo one! Handsome set his jaw and pulled his chauffeur's cap down over his eyes so far it was like it was a superhero mask.

"Come on, Miss Billie. We've got to go help the lady now. She's going to need our help in a minute. See over there?"

Baby, take all of me.

He began to run, run toward the danger, toward the fire. Someone had lit it again, and that was a *dead someone*. Soon the fire would spread across the Ramparts, as it did so often during this time of year. But usually folks weren't here to see it.

They was about to see it now, though.

Oh, yeah, Miss Billie! They's all about to see it!

Chapter Nineteen – Avery

I clicked off the television and headed downstairs to grab a bite to eat. Grandmother Margaret's storytelling had once again grabbed my imagination and held it captive. I was foolish to think I'd tackle both Vertie's diaries and these videos in the space of an afternoon, but I was certainly giving it the "old college try." Margaret had a knack for telling stories. For the hundredth time, I wondered how she could know any of this. Were these stories that a family member passed on to her? A matrone, perhaps? Who would I ask to verify her tales?

I foraged through the refrigerator and found a cling-wrap-covered plate that contained a sandwich, a sliver of pickle and a small cup of fruit salad. It had a sticky note with my name and a friendly smiley face on it. How thoughtful of Robin to leave this for me! I snagged it and intended to head back upstairs to finish the videos. I heard voices nearby, probably some of the housekeeping staff, so I didn't think much of it. The young women were always tidying up something, and I could smell wood polish. I heard Robin's laugh and breathed a sigh of relief. Thank goodness it was a voice from the land of the living.

"Miss Dufresne, may I help you with something?" I yelped in surprise. Pepper stood in my foyer. She watched me unsmilingly, her hands in her cardigan pockets.

"No, I don't think so. Is there something you need, Pepper?"

"I want to talk to you. If you have a minute." She closed the side door and waited for me to answer.

"Sure, let's talk." *Yes, let's get this out in the open. Maybe there is some way we can come to a peaceable agreement.* "Come into the dining room. I don't think there's anyone in there." I led the way as a feeling of dread washed over me. This wasn't how I wanted to spend the rest of my day.

I put the plate down on the long wooden table and invited her to sit across from me. I left the chair at the head of the table empty, hoping that would help her feel more comfortable.

Pepper wore her shoulder-length hair up in a comb today. The hairstyle looked sloppy on some women, but it looked elegant on her. It suddenly occurred to me that she looked very much like Miss Anne. In fact, she could have been a slightly younger version— down to the pearl earrings and the expensive lipstick. Yes, I could see the resemblance now.

"What can I help you with?"

"Summer advised me to come see you. She said that I should tell you how I feel, that you would under-stand. That you were a reasonable woman. Well, here I am."

"She's right. I like to think I'm reasonable. My door is always open to family, and I want to hear how you feel, Pepper. Is there anything wrong? Something specific you want to discuss?" Pretending I didn't know she wanted me out as matrone was proving more difficult than I could have imagined. My blood was boiling.

"Yes. There is." She leaned forward, her hand on the table as if she needed to steady herself—or restrain herself. I couldn't be sure which. Pepper was a slight woman, but she was what Vertie would call "scrappy." Despite her fine handbag and gold rings, I had no doubt she'd be ready to rumble if the occasion called for it. I hoped that wasn't today. I didn't think I was up for mixing it up with a relative.

This might be a good time to take the high road. "If this is about the board meeting, Pepper, I'd like to put your mind at ease. I have since learned that I broke with tradition by speaking out like I did. However, as far as I know, I haven't broken any rules. I'm sure you understand that I'm new to all this."

"Oh, I don't think time is a luxury you have right now. Time is running out. For you, at least."

"What do you mean?" I could hardly believe what I was hearing. "Are you threatening me?"

Pepper leaned even closer and with a bleak smile said, "I am not the threat here. I came to warn you." The old Avery would have told her off and tossed her out, but I wasn't that woman anymore. I reminded myself to be calm and remember that Pepper had quite a bit of pull on the board. If I could swing her to my side, make her see reason, perhaps I could build inroads into the more doubtful factions of the family? Why couldn't they believe I only wanted to help?

"You can't expect that Miss Anne and I would do things the same way, but I have nothing but this family's interests at heart. I hope you believe that. I want to see Dolly Jane and children like her get the treatment they need. Our family can do so much good! Let's put any differences aside and do some good together. Let's build that medical clinic in the bayou. I know that means something to you. Let's fund more scholarships. What can we do to work together, Pepper? I know we can do great things."

"Such nice words, but it's not your agenda that I'm here about."

"Oh? Then what may I help you with?"

"The money, the affluence, that's always the bait. But it's not about that. It's about you, Avery. You are in danger, although you don't seem to know it. Someone should have told you—they should have given you a choice! It's wrong to do this to you without warning."

"Danger? Warning about what?"

"You should go back where you came from, Avery. You should hop back in that shiny silver car and go back to Atlanta." Her voice was hypnotic, smooth, like she wanted to convince me to do just what she said. I supposed she meant to soothe my nerves, but all it did was tick me off. I'd always had a mind of my own.

My appetite vanished quickly, and I pushed the plate aside. "I see. And is that your opinion, Pepper, or do you all feel this way?"

"I know you have questions. You're bound to. You are a smart girl, but smarts aren't enough to face what's coming your way. You will have to make a decision. Who will you pick?" With a sad sigh, she opened the palm of her hand. She wore neat gloves, the kind that women in the forties wore. I hadn't noticed them before, but they were a soft pink, almost her skin color. "Take my hand."

I stared at it and then at her. What was this about? "Are you a palm reader? Because I'm not into that." I glanced at her other hand but saw nothing there. No weapons. No blunt objects.

"Please, take my hand, Avery. I can provide you with the answers you are looking for."

"How? Are you taking me somewhere?"

"No. We aren't going anywhere. I'm not going to hurt you. Take my hand, Avery. Take my hand and you'll see what I see. You'll know it all. I hope you are truly ready to know the truth."

I shrugged at the crazy lady sitting across from me. *Fine. I'll take her hand and then she'll be gone. If it gets rid of her, what's the harm? I'm tired, and I have a ton more research to do.*

Without a smile or even a remotely kind expression, I put my hand in hers. Instantly I experienced a strange detachment. It reminded me of getting nitrous oxide at the dentist. Afterwards my mind had felt cloudy, and I hadn't enjoyed the experience. I hated feeling out of control.

And at this moment I had no doubt—nothing that was about to happen to me was within my control.

Chapter Twenty – Avery

"Now repeat after me, Avery. I am the bell, and you are the song. I am the heart, but you are the blood..."

My lips trembled as I whispered the words.

"No, louder, Avery. Say them louder. He has to hear you say the words or he can't come."

My stomach did a flip, and I glanced up at the older girl with some puzzlement. I didn't know why I resisted speaking the words, maybe because she wanted me to so badly. "I don't want to make the spell. You do it. Why don't you say them? You do it and I'll watch." Even that seemed repulsive, but I was ready to compromise at this point.

"Because. It doesn't work that way. Are you going to say them or not?"

"Not. I'm going home." I picked up my book bag and slung it over my shoulders.

Quick as lightning, Rita Faye was on her feet and standing between me and the door. The girl was a full foot taller than me, and it bothered me that she knew how much it intimidated me. I didn't back down. "Get out of the way, Rita, or I'll punch you in the gut." I showed her my fist and shoved out my chin.

"Just try it. Say the damn words, Avery Dufresne."

Rita Faye thought swearing would intimidate me even more. She didn't know me too well. I could swear way better than she could, I'd been living on this Navy base a lot longer than her. I'd picked up all sorts of interesting words, and I wasn't afraid to use any of them.

"Go on and admit it. You are scared! Scared of the Skelly Man! Ha ha! I told you you believed in the Skelly Man!" Rita Faye mocked me with a twisted expression. Her ugly brown hair sprung out from her ponytail unevenly; she looked like she hadn't brushed it in a month of Sundays. But then her hair always looked bad after a day at school. I'd wanted to be her friend because she didn't have any. I knew why now. She was mean and pushy and liked to boss people around. I was done trying to be her friend. I would much rather be alone.

"Get out of the way or I'll scream. If you think the Skelly Man is mean, just wait until you meet my grandmother!" I was ready to cry now, but not because I was afraid of any stupid ghost. I was afraid that I wouldn't be allowed to go home; that I would be away from Vertie forever. That frightened me. Rita Faye slapped herself against the closed door.

"You aren't going anywhere, Avery Dufresne. You say the words, and then you can go. If you don't say the words you aren't my friend and you'll be stuck in here forever."

"No, I won't!" I screamed, unafraid that her grumpy father would hear me.

"Nobody can hear you. They are all drinking in the garage and listening to music, stupid. Now say it!" She pinched me, and I screamed in pain as I stepped back. I eyed the window, but it was closed tight and there was no way I could break free. Besides, I didn't think I could handle falling from the second floor. It was too high up.

Then I felt heat rising within me. It started in my gut and then began to flare out to my fingers and toes. I thought maybe I'd cry, maybe I'd throw up. Something was building, and it was strong and dangerous. I'd never experienced this before. "Get. Out. Of. The. Way," I warned her as I struggled to breathe. My backpack felt like a hundred pounds on my back. My head felt heavy—even my skin felt heavy. Something bad was about to happen. Real bad.

"Get. Out. Of. The. Way..." she mocked me, and then suddenly she slammed back against the wood and flattened against the door. Her legs twisted, her feet tapped one another and I watched her urinate on herself. She made a horrible gurgling sound, and her head twisted in a weird position as her body lifted from the ground. Her feet weren't even touching the floor! She couldn't move—she couldn't speak!

"Rita?" My mind asked the question, but I couldn't speak either. Suddenly the door swung open and I ran from the room like a coward, leaving her plastered across the door.

"Vertie! Vertie!" I whispered to my brain as I ran. The strange heaviness lifted from me, and I kept running across the scraggly, dirty carpet, down the stairs and out the dingy white front door. By the time I made it to the corner of the street, Rita Faye was screaming; I could hear her in her room. I kept running.

Tears filled my eyes, and I felt Pepper's hand squeeze mine. I thought she would let go, but she didn't. I'd actually forgotten she was there, that I was here. I think she said something else to me, but I couldn't hear what it was. The room we sat in became cloudy again.

And I wasn't me anymore. I was no longer Avery.

I was Anne.

"Now, say the words, Annie. Be a good girl and say the words."

"I don't believe in magic, Grandmother. I don't want to say them."

"Fine, then I'll ask Vertie to do it."

I was reluctant—I wasn't jealous of Vertie or worried that I'd lose my status as the favorite grandchild. I wanted to protect Vertie from the bad thing, although my little sister did not believe in it. How could I show her?

"All right, Grandmother. If it makes you happy." I twisted my fingers behind my back. Crossed fingers

meant you could break a promise. Even to a grand-mother. "I am the bell, and you are the song. I am the heart, but you are the blood. Together, we two. Al-ways. We are one soul."

"That's good, Annie. Now say it again. Say it louder, dear."

As she spoke, my skin began to crawl and my vision became blurry. I was only twelve, but I knew this was wrong. I knew my priest would disapprove of this. I didn't understand why, but I knew.

"No more, Grandmother. No more, okay?" Grand-mother Margaret grabbed my hands now and then held me by the wrists as she pulled me close. No. She wasn't going to let me go. I sighed under the sudden feeling of weightiness, as if someone had put a heavy robe on me, a robe I couldn't see and hadn't been ex-pecting to wear. And didn't want to wear. The robe made me feel sad, kind of sick. "Please." I began to cry softly.

"Almost done, girl. Almost there." I could smell Grandmother Margaret's stale coffee breath, and I continued to cry. She said the words, and I repeated them. My fingers were no longer crossed because she held my wrists tight now. She whispered the rest of the words in my ear. My mouth worked, but I didn't want to say the words. I didn't want to! I couldn't! Now I knew what the priest had said was true. Mortal sins were real!

"Now! Say it again! Stop struggling, my dear."

"Grandmother! What are you doing to Anne?" Vertie stormed into the room and pushed her way between us. She was so small, so petite, but no one had a stronger will than Vertie Lee Dufresne.

"Mind your own business, Vertie. Go outside and play with your brother."

Vertie's plain face darkened with anger. She scowled at Grandmother Margaret and wagged her finger at her, as if she were the grown-up and Grandmother Margaret the child. "No! You leave her alone. Look! You've made her cry, and she has bruises on her wrists. Come on, let's go, Anne."

Vertie snatched me away, and we left the stuffy upstairs room behind. I breathed a sigh of relief as I practically fell behind her. Our grandmother's companion and housemaid, Antoinette, stepped out into the hallway and peered at us disapprovingly but didn't try to stop us. Where had she come from? The Mirror Room? I walked down the stairs with Vertie, but I knew it was too late. I'd said the words, I'd spoken enough of the spell. I wore the heavy, invisible coat now forever.

And I would see the Lovely Man.

I was his now.

***

I laid my head on the table and cried. Pepper released my hand and shuffled through her purse for some tissue. Shoving it in my hand she said, "Now you know. You know what they don't want you to know."

I didn't think. I cried. I cried until I couldn't cry anymore. "I'd forgotten about Rita Faye. I thought I dreamed that whole thing. Who was she?"

"Oh, I think you know."

"I don't know if I understand this. How could you know what happened to me? And why did I see Anne? I didn't say the words."

"You don't have to say the words, Avery. The spirit always comes for the matrone. It was just a coincidence that day with Rita Faye. But you saw what happened to Anne. She had no choice. And as cruel as it was, she left you with no choice either. Her daughters died, and she rejected Asner's child, for whatever reason. She put the ring on your finger knowing that he'd come for you."

"What does he want?"

"He wants you. He wants his *soul mate*. He's bound to the ring."

"The ring I can't get off my finger. Why would she do this to me, knowing that I would be...haunted by

Ambrose?" The very speaking of his name made the air shimmer around me.

"I don't know. I can't imagine why she would give it to anyone. Why not die with it on her finger? Who knows? I think the cancer made her mind weak. Or maybe she didn't want to give up the money. The legend is that's the trade-off, your love and your soul for the fortune. And this family, they couldn't care less about your soul, Avery. If you think that they're your friends, that they love you, think again." We both pretended that we didn't hear footsteps above us. Pacing back and forth, as if he were there and waiting for me.

"Summer? Reed? Mitchell? They all know?"

"Everyone knows the legend, but I daresay many don't believe it. But those three, they believe. They've all seen him, with Miss Anne. At Thorn Hill."

"So if I reject him, I lose the money and the family loses the fortune? And what else? Will he kill me?"

"That's what they say, but no one has ever rejected him. Not as far as I know, anyway. Will he kill you?" She tapped her lip with her finger. "I don't know. I think he fancies he loves you because when he sees you, he sees Susanna."

"Why didn't Vertie tell me all this?"

"Oh, I think you know the answer to that. She wanted to protect you. A fool's errand, but she had to try, didn't she? I would have. I loved Vertie. She was a good woman, always had been, but she was naïve to believe that simply hiding you away would keep you from the Dufresne curse."

A loud crash upstairs had us both on our feet. "I'd better go." She reached for her handbag and touched my arm. "No matter what happens, you do what is right for you, Avery."

"Thank you, Pepper. I'll do my best. And yes, you'd better go." Cold entered the room suddenly; it was so cold that I wanted to wrap myself in a blanket. Eager for her to leave, I walked her to the front door and we parted ways without another word. She'd taken a huge risk coming here.

Now what was I going to do? I heard another noise, this time coming from the dining room. Something crashed; it sounded like the chandelier falling again, only I was in a different house. I walked to the door, but the dining room was so cold now I didn't dare go in. The cold took my breath away.

Come to me now...

Surely I imagined that! I walked backward away from the dining room—away from the voice. And then I heard the whispers, many voices. They practically swirled around me, threatening to swallow me. Smother me. Take me away.

"Who's there?" I called into the dark room in front of me.

Susanna...

"I'm not Susanna!"

I watched in horror as a thick, dark shadow slid out under the door and pooled in front of me. I whimpered as it began to gather in a heap just a few feet from me. The gathering of darkness climbed higher, just a foot, then two, and finally the thing was my height and a slow swirling motion began.

This is going to be bad. This is going to be so bad. What do I do? My mind couldn't comprehend what I witnessed. And then I heard Vertie's voice whispering in my ear.

"Avery, run! Run now!"

Her voice didn't soothe me. It ratcheted my emotions to new, terrifying heights, and I raced toward the front door. In one fell swoop I snatched my keys off the table and with nervous fingers began to punch numbers on my phone.

I could think of only one person who could help me.

Chapter Twenty-One – Jessica

"Stop a minute, Jeffrey!" I grabbed his hand and pulled him down next to me.

"But there's a fire!"

"No, there isn't. Look. It's gone." The burst of flame had disappeared completely. There wasn't a single spark or ember left behind.

"What the hell?" He squatted down beside me and asked, "How can that be?"

"Keep your voice down." Yeah, that was pretty foolish. I didn't believe for a second there was anyone out here besides us, but Becker took his role as our unofficial "debunker" seriously. He wanted to investigate, and I needed to record it. To my surprise, as soon as I pulled my phone out of my pocket, it began to ring. I just about jumped out of my skin.

"Hold on. Wait! This is Avery!" With a cold shiver I answered her call. "Hi, Avery. This is Jessica."

"Where are you?"

"Um, on the Ramparts. Right off the main road."

"I'm on the way."

I could hear the fear in her voice. All was not well. "Is there something wrong at Sugar Hill?"

"Yes, I heard a crashing sound upstairs, and my dining room is freezing. I can't go back in there."

"Go outside right now and stay there. We're coming to you."

"All right, but hurry up. I'm sitting in my car."

"Okay, be there in a few minutes." I stared at Becker, but before I could tell him anything, our fearless leader and Megan walked up. I didn't point out that Mike had pink lipstick on his neck.

"I'll let you tell him the good news," Beck said.

"What are you two doing out here? Getting a head start?" Mike didn't hide his aggravation.

"We saw something that looked like a ball of fire. Over there. But it's gone now."

"Where? In the ruins?" Mike pointed toward the old foundation where we'd fixed the camera.

"Yeah, but that's not all. Avery is having a problem at the house. She wants us to come over there and investigate. She's got a cold spot and some bangs. Seems like we stirred up something."

"Oh Lord. What now, Jessica?"

"Nothing. I haven't done anything, Megan."

Mike slid his MHP hat off his head and back on. It was his go-to move when he was aggravated. "We can't abandon this spot. I've already told the channel we'd be out here tonight—they will be expecting some footage."

"Yeah, but it is Sugar Hill. You know that's the real prize here. Why not let me and Beck go over there? You can keep James, Megan and the other guy."

"Fine, but be thorough. And no going rogue, Jess. If you sense something or see something, keep it to yourself. At least until we can all go over the evidence. No spontaneous reporting to the client."

"I had no other plans, Mike."

"I mean it, no more going rogue."

"I didn't go rogue! You make it sound like I did it on purpose so they could find the bodies. I guess you think I stuffed them in there too? Are we really going to stand out here and argue in the woods?" His criticism hurt my feelings more than I cared to admit.

The leaves crunched behind me, and I heard Megan talking on her cell phone. "Great. See you then!" she said. Then she hung up and beamed at us. "Hey, guys, Summer just called me. She's coming out to do an interview tonight. Has some cool details to share about the Ramparts. And she's so photogenic. This will definitely make good television." She had a proud grin on her face, but I was more than puzzled. Why would Summer suddenly want to come out here? I was keenly aware that we'd gotten ourselves in the middle of some type of familial struggle, but I couldn't figure it all out. I wondered if the others had any clue.

"That's strange timing. Jessica just got a call from Avery. She's heading back to Sugar Hill with Becker."

Becker huffed and said, "Come on." His voice was kind of whiny, like a teenager's. "We need to spend some time investigating this location. We've got the equipment up, and our time is limited. I'd rather stay here."

"Only because Summer is coming out," I said disapprovingly. Was he deliberately trying to keep us from investigating the house? "Look, you do what you want, but I have to go. Avery needs help."

"Jess, what did I just say about going rogue?"

"Guys! Cut it out. I'll go with Jess, and you and Becker stay here, do the interview and conduct the investigation as we planned. Chances are it's just Avery's nerves or something. I mean, that's to be expected when people find skeletons in your basement. We'll check it out and come back when we're through."

"Well, you won't be disappointed here," I said. "We've already seen a fireball. Check the footage. I recorded it." I felt relieved that Megan supported my decision. I was eager to help Avery, if I could. If we could.

Megan smiled and slid her arm in mine. *And why are we suddenly BFFs? Because she and Mike made up?*

"All right, you two, but be careful. Grab some gear and get going."

"Roger that," Megan said with a perky smile, and we scrambled into the van to grab the usual toys. Then she slid behind the wheel of the truck. It smelled like musky cameramen, but they didn't give us a hard time when we evicted them. It was time to go to work anyway. Just as we turned onto the sloping driveway of Sugar Hill, she asked me, "What do you think is going on here, Jessica?"

"To put it bluntly, I think it's what the old folks would call a reckoning." Fortunately she did not ask me to explain myself. I wasn't sure I could, but it was as good a description as I could muster.

"Great. Sounds promising." She put the truck in park and said, "Since Miss Dufresne reached out to you, I think it's best if you take the lead in the conversation. I'll hang back and back you up."

"There she is." I grabbed the small duffel bag and met Avery at the back of her Lexus. I'd watched her on the news. Not religiously, because I wasn't a big fan of the news, but I'd seen her enough to know she didn't get shaken easily. And now here she was, shaken to the core.

She took a deep breath. "Okay, full disclosure. Ever since I moved here, there's been weird crap happening."

"Weird crap?" Megan asked. So much for letting me take the lead.

"Yeah, weird." Avery paused her pacing. She had her hands on her hips and was obviously disturbed. Her usually neat hair was not so neat now, she didn't have any shoes on and she was visibly trembling.

"Okay, Avery. Well, we're here," I stepped in. "Why don't we go back inside? You don't have shoes on, and Megan and I are here now. Do you feel safe doing that, or should we sit in the truck for a few minutes?"

She chewed on her thumbnail and sighed loudly. "God, I'm being such a wimp. I called you because a black shadow from the dining room gathered up and stood in front of me. It called me Susanna. Something really bad is going to happen, and I don't know what to do."

"Hey, it's okay, Avery. You aren't alone now." I didn't touch her. Avery was a sensitive, like me, and from what I'd gathered in the short time I'd known her, she didn't have a clue about managing it.

"All right, let's go in." We walked inside, and immediately I got the distinct impression, for the third time, that whatever was here didn't want me to know it was here. Like he—no, they—didn't want me to see them.

Without saying anything to Megan or Avery, I began to talk to the spirits. "I know you are here, and so does Avery. There's no sense in hiding now." Megan stared at me and then snapped to attention. She grabbed the duffel bag and foraged for her investigative tools. She held an EMF reader and began sweeping it around. She handed me the EVP recorder, but I didn't use it yet. I couldn't move too quickly because I didn't want to frighten Avery even more.

The spirit didn't answer, and after a minute or two of pacing the foyer I asked, "You know who's here, don't you, Avery? Tell us, please, so we can help you."

She didn't answer me right away. She was listening to the house creak and pop in the humidity.

"This might be the only way," I added.

"Well, I don't guess I have anything to lose at this point."

I could tell she was about to blow my mind.

Chapter Twenty-Two – Avery

"Jessica, the truth is that this ring I wear...wait. You can't record this, Megan!" She frowned at me, but I wasn't going to budge. She nodded and begrudgingly put her video equipment away. I raised my hand and wiggled my ring finger, ignoring the surge of warmth it emitted. "I'm the matrone, the symbolic leader of my family. That's what this ring is supposed to signify, but it's more than that. It attracts a spirit—a spirit that is looking for his soul mate."

"So that ring is like a power object? Who is this ghost?" Megan was immediately intrigued.

"Ambrose. His name is Ambrose." Eyes were on me. I could feel them staring, bearing into me. And not just living human eyes. I swallowed and continued, "He was Chase Dufresne's cousin and the lover of Chase's wife, Susanna Dufresne, although it's a bit more complicated than that. I think it's him. He's the one haunting me."

Jessica's pretty face scrunched up in disgust. "Why would you wear that ring? Take it off, Avery." She reached for it, but I shook my head.

"It won't come off. I've tried everything except have it cut off. I just can't bring myself to do that. I guess I'll have to. That might be the only way to get rid of him." Jessica held my hand, closed her eyes briefly and then released me. If she sensed anything, she didn't tell me. "He—I don't want to say his name too often because he can hear me—he believes the wearer of his ring is his soul mate. It belonged to Susanna. Her mother put a kind of curse on it."

Megan laughed. "Are you sure? So this ghost believes you are Susanna? Is this a true story or just a family legend?"

"I don't know what he believes. But the story is true, and I have recorded family history to back it up. According to my great-great-grandmother Margaret, many Dufresne husbands have died under suspicious circumstances. Or at the very least gone mad."

Suddenly I understood what was happening to Jamie. It was the curse working on him. It was Ambrose trying to keep us apart. That had to be it. Why else would Jamie's personality flip so wildly? And where was he? God, I hoped he was all right.

"This spirit is very…possessive. So much so that he's a danger to the people around me. I can't have that."

Megan leaned against the wall, her arms crossed stiffly in front of her. Her expression made me even more nervous. I wondered what was eating her.

I continued, "*He* was the lover of Susanna Dufresne; he seduced her into betraying her husband and even had her declare that she was his soul mate. He was murdered during the fire on the Ramparts. I don't know who set the fire, not for sure, but some of the women and girls in my family have seen him. They call him the Lovely Man."

"Could it be a familiar spirit?" Jessica pondered aloud.

"Like from the Bible?" asked Megan as she tinkered with her handheld devices.

"I guess, but the existence of these beings has been recorded in many places. They're entities that are attached to the family, usually through spells or curses. Some are nasty, evil spirits, and others are less dangerous. One such case I've studied features a ghost that consistently appears in family photos, but..."

"But what?" I asked as Jessica strolled around and stopped at the bottom of the stairs. She stared up the stairs as if she could see something we couldn't. Maybe she could.

Without even taking her eyes off the door, she answered me in a flat voice, "The ring disturbs me. We have to find a way to... Can anyone else hear that?"

The room fell silent. I didn't hear anything at first, until I walked to the bottom of the stairs. At the first boom I practically jumped out of my skin. It was the unmistakable sound of a door slamming. I wasn't sure where it was coming from, maybe the Angel Gallery.

"Turn out the lights, Jessica," Megan said. "I think we need to go up."

I glanced over my shoulder at the dining room. "But what I saw was in there. Shouldn't we start in there?" I heard the sound too, but I was stalling. Even though I had experienced more than my share of ghostly encounters at Sugar Hill, this felt different. The presence in the house felt heavy, dark and determined to reach me. I couldn't fathom the change, except perhaps that the opening of the basement and the revelation that two women had been walled up and left to die here had fueled whatever already called this place home.

As if to answer me, more slamming and scratching echoed above us.

"Fine, but why are we turning out the lights?" Megan had lost her mind if she thought I wanted to investigate in the dark.

"Trust me," she said as she pulled a flashlight out of her pocket and flicked it on. "They like the dark. We'll get more of a response if we limit the amount of light we use."

"Great," I whispered.

Another door on the second floor, farther away, now slammed shut. Someone was trying to avoid us—or lure us onward. I had a suspicion that it was a dead someone and not a member of the housekeeping staff.

Together the three of us started walking up the stairs, and I began preparing myself for what we might find. "It could be one of the housekeepers. Dinah pretty much does whatever the hell she wants. I never know where she's going to turn up."

Megan paused on the steps. "Are you saying you don't want us to go up there? We don't have to. We just want to help."

"No. Let's do this."

As we reached the top of the wide wooden staircase, she stopped and peered into the darkness. "Jessica, what are you feeling? Anything?" Her voice sounded confident, and I took comfort in that.

"Not much yet. What about you, Avery?"

"Yes...someone is here, but I don't know who."

"Are you okay to move forward?" Jessica handed me a flashlight. I pushed the rubber button on the end and shined the bright LED light in front of me.

"I'm ready. I think it's coming from the Angel Gallery. Let's go." I took a deep breath and flicked off the hall light.

It was now or never.

Chapter Twenty-Three – Summer

"Make a choice, Summer," Danforth's voice boomed through the phone. "You either get rid of her now or you don't. Let me just make you aware of what's at stake here. If you don't get her out of the way tonight, you'll never have our support again. This was your idea, and now it's time to deliver. I'm putting my neck on the line for you—for the family. Show us you are the true matrone. Get rid of her!" I'd hung up the phone without answering him. What else was there to say?

I tapped on the steering wheel nervously, wondering what the hell to do next. If I called Reed I'd have to explain to him how I'd lobbied the board for a vote of no confidence in Avery. How in the beginning I wanted to take what was mine!

Until I got to know Avery. Until I believed in her. Until I knew exactly what it would cost to change the status quo. I wasn't willing to pay the price, was I?

Yes, I still dreamed of Ambrose and wanted him, wanted to be his, even though he had not chosen me—I wanted that more than my next breath. But not enough to murder.

With no plan, I decided to follow my instincts. I'd go to the Ramparts. I'd talk to Becker; maybe somehow I could convince him to do the dirty work for me.

You can't do that, Summer! You'd still be guilty!

It was as if Aunt Anne were in the car with me. I grabbed my flashlight and scurried down the well-hidden path that would lead me to the My Haunted Plantation crew. I couldn't explain it, but I had to go. I had to be there. I lied to myself and said it was because of Becker, but that wasn't it. Not in the least. It was because Ambrose was going to be there. And I needed to know why. Why had he rejected me? Why had he cast me aside for Avery?

A day of reckoning was coming to Ambrose. He must pay for what he'd done.

Yes, what he's done to us all, Summer. He is an evil man to love us and leave us so.

I paused on the sandy pathway. Who said that? Why was I hearing a woman's voice out here? And how did she know my name?

"Hello?" I called, half expecting someone to answer.

"Hey, Summer! We're over here."

I saw Becker down the path a bit, and I jogged toward him. I glanced over my shoulder once but saw nothing. No women stalking me and calling me by name.

"Thought you'd changed your mind. It's really good of you to come out and offer your insights. It's going to help us a lot. I am glad I suggested it—and if you don't mind too much, could you mention that to

Mike? I'd like him to know that this was my idea. It'll give me a little street cred."

"What?" I asked, staring up at him.

"Are you okay? Did you get stoned on the way here or something? You look out of it."

"I'm not sure what's going on with me. I'm hearing voices. Someone called my name."

"That's cool. Let me get my audio recorder. Maybe we can pick it up again."

"No, let's go to the Ramparts. I have to see him—I mean see the place."

"All right, we've had some action already. Camera Three picked up a strange fire burst that came up from the ground. We've checked it out, and it's not gas or anything flammable. Just good old air around here."

"Yeah, fire bursts are bad." I wore my Keds, blue jeans and a thick jacket, but I was still freaking cold. "Put your arm around me, Becker. I'm freezing."

"Sure, but I have to warn you, you're putting yourself in danger. Doing it in the woods is on my bucket list."

I stopped walking and waved my flashlight in his face. No, he wasn't Ambrose, no trace of him there. "I'm sorry to tell you that you are out of luck tonight.

I'm not here just to give an interview. I am hoping you can help me reach out to one particular ghost. His name is Ambrose. He died in the Ramparts fire about two hundred years ago."

He smiled playfully. "Oh, so that's who you were dreaming about last night. And I was jealous of a ghost. What a dumbass!"

I didn't joke around with him but just kept walking. Soon I could see the lights of the black MHP van in the distance. We were getting close. Then suddenly Handsome Cheever stepped out into the pathway, his hat pulled down so far over his eyes that I was surprised he could see us at all.

"Don't go, Miss Summer. Don't go, please."

"You don't know what you're talking about, Handsome. Get lost."

"I know what you're going to do, and it won't work. He won't take you; he's already chosen Avery. You have to let him go, ma'am, or he is going to kill you. Kill you dead."

"What?" Becker shook his head. "Who's going to kill Summer? I'll kick his ass!"

"You ain't kickin' no ghost's ass. He'll kill you dead too just for messin' with him. He's an old ghost, and he's been around these parts for a long time. Now what you got in that bag, Miss Summer?"

"Never you mind, Handsome! Now get out of the way!" I pushed his shoulder, but he barely moved. I slipped by him and continued toward my destination. Wherever that was. I walked past the MHP van with Becker running behind me.

Becker shouted, "Get the equipment, Mike, and come with me! She's going to do something crazy!" Mike grabbed bags of gear and followed us as I walked down the narrow path to the center of the Ramparts.

Then I saw her. There was no doubt she was a ghost. To my surprise, she looked like me. She had long blond hair that fell in curls. She had a trim figure, which I could see quite clearly under that fluttering white dress. I think Becker saw her too because he gasped and began waving his K2 around.

She spoke to my mind so only I could hear her. *You want him to suffer too. He rejected you too! You know how it feels to be loved by Ambrose and have him take that love away. I could not have that.* She stepped closer, and the smell of burning hair began to fill my nostrils. *No, I could not have that at all. But I took care of it. He'll never be with her now. No more Susanna for him. I did my part, Summer. Now it's time you did yours.* Suddenly the girl, Coquette—I knew her name as surely as I knew mine—changed. There was no more blond hair and soft white skin. No more white dress. She was burnt beyond belief, her hair melted to her skin, her nose and lips nonexistent, her burnt fingers twisted and her nude body swollen. I screamed and screamed again, falling backwards and scrambling away as she stepped toward me.

"Don't run from me. I am you and you are me. You must finish it, Summer. You must burn them all. Use it, use the lighter, burn them all!"

"No! I won't do it! I won't murder anyone!" Suddenly Handsome stood beside me. He tossed a handful of salt on the burnt corpse, and she began to steam and melt away into the forest floor. She screamed from the pain but never stopped reaching for me. Handsome tossed handful after handful of salt around me to protect me. I did as he told me and stayed in the circle until the place went still again.

And it was still now. So still that I wondered if there was anything living here.

Suddenly flames shot up from the ground. First one, then another. Coquette wasn't through with us yet! The ghost fire burned invisible buildings on both sides of the street that appeared before me. I saw the world in the 1800s, and it was all on fire. Then I realized that somewhere in that world was Ambrose—he was alive, and if I wanted to be with him, now was the time. I would make him see I was right for him. He would not need anyone but me. I would be all things for him. And I would die to be with him.

Just then, Handsome grabbed my shoulders. "You ain't gonna die today. Miss Billie is singing hard over you. You ain't going to die today! Be still, child. Be still. That desire will pass. It's a kind of magic, a bad magic, from that ring you played with as a child. The ring cast a spell on you even though you wasn't able to claim it. No, you have to renounce it."

"No! That would mean I would never..."

"And you never will, Miss Summer. It's not you he wants..."

I cried and looked up into his eyes. I heard Becker talking, but I ignored him. He understood less than nothing. I didn't have time to explain my life to him, nor did I want to. "What do I have to do?" It pained me to even ask the question.

"Say these words and mean them with your heart: 'I renounce you, Ambrose Dufresne....'"

My lips trembled as I tried. "I renounce you...Ambrose Dufresne...." My heart was banging in my chest. I didn't want to do this, but I trusted Handsome. I knew he would help me if he could.

"...and I renounce the ring and its magic. I am not your wife or your soul mate. I am nothing to you but a distant relative."

I tearfully repeated the words, and suddenly Ambrose appeared. He wasn't the fine, handsome young man I remembered but a corpse, a horrible-looking thing that I could never imagine desiring.

"He is letting you see him for who he is because he wants you to be free, Summer. He wants you to be free."

I cried on Handsome's chest and refused to look at Ambrose anymore. Finally, I felt the air warm and the stench dissipate.

"Let's go home now, Miss Dufresne. Miss Billie has stopped singing. She's all done. All is well now. We will be safe, I promise you, we will be safe. At least for a while."

Chapter Twenty-Four – Avery & Susanna

Avery

Jessica and Megan passed me protectively as another door slammed. Or was it the same door? It couldn't be the door to the Mirror Room, which was already closed. But this door, it shut over and over again. It was farther away. Impossibly far.

"Ambrose, are you here? We're not here to harm you. We just want to talk. Avery wants to talk to you." The three of us lingered in the hall, Megan waving her handheld scanner, the lights flashing from light green to deep green. Jessica had an audio device in her hand.

Jessica whispered to me, "If he talks to us the light will flash. You can't always hear spirit responses with the naked ear." I didn't care about the details. I just wanted to get this over with. I wanted it all over with. Maybe I should go back to Atlanta and just leave all this behind. But that was just a dream. I had to face this; I couldn't run from it. I wore the ring.

"Ambrose, if you are with us, just speak into this red light. We'll be able to hear you...did you hear that?" The sound of retreating footsteps lured the investigators further down the hall. "It came from over here," Jessica whispered. Apparently she hadn't noticed that the door to the Mirror Room now stood open.

And soft candlelight now fluttered enticingly from behind the door. At least I thought it was candlelight...

My flashlight dimmed significantly and then went out completely. I heard Jessica say my name, but it was as if she were talking to me underwater. I couldn't make it out.

All I could do was walk toward the light...and then I saw him. Standing near the candle, with his hand on the shiny oak table, was Chase Dufresne. He extended his other hand to me...with all my heart, I accepted it.

***

Susanna Serene

It had been a full three days since Chase showed up on the doorstep at Thorn Hill. His wound wasn't as bad as Ingrid and I first believed, but even the doctor agreed that his blood loss remained a most serious concern.

He had no visitors, except the sheriff who merely inquired about his status. The ugly little man even refused to come inside the house, discussing it all on the front porch. I told him what I knew. That I'd had no contact with Chase for nearly two years until this unwanted visit. Yes, he lived, but recovery would be a slow process.

Thankfully no one else came by to ask after him. Ambrose stayed away, and the town was abuzz with the scandal. That first night, I watched my husband's pale sleeping face until the wee hours of the morning. This was the face of the man who had rejected me, who had shamed me before his friends—and his second wife. Here was the man who would not claim me but also would not let me go. Chase had done even worse than that. He left our daughter with Etienne. Even if he hated me with all his being, he should have cared for her.

"How could I ever have loved you?" He did not stir— he did not answer. And what would he say? Just the night before he'd begged for my forgiveness. Would I forgive him? In the beginning I said no, never. But after days of care and attention, and as my desperation rose, desperation to see him healed, I felt my heart of stone soften. And that I didn't want. I began to sling down whiskey in between my ministrations. I'd abandoned my duties at my shop and most days sent Ingrid instead. And in all this time, Chase had awoken only once and was so fevered that he thought I was his sister, Regina.

"Regina, dear. I knew you were not dead. I heard you calling me, but I couldn't find you. I looked, sister. Where have you been? Regina?" I calmed him, and he fell asleep again, lost in his mad world. For the first time in so much longer than I could remember, I prayed fervently.

Chase's hair had grown darker; he wore it longer now. His dark blond sideburns made him appear older than he was—I knew he was a full two years younger than me. Gleaming from his neck was a golden chain and crucifix; it was a delicate Spanish working. I had given it to him as a wedding present. I touched it but withdrew my hand when he stirred. Eventually weariness overcame me and I fell asleep. For some reason I dreamed of Sulli and her wide eyes, her lips mouthing a secret I should have remembered but couldn't. I woke to a light tapping on the guest room door. My back was stiff, and I was embarrassed to find that I had been lying across the corner of the bed. It was Ingrid, of course. She was up early, dressed neatly and holding a folded letter.

"This came for you, Miss Susanna. The man who delivered it is waiting downstairs for your reply. I have seen him before; he stays with Coquette. One of her servants, he is. So you can guess who this is from."

I shoved the loose hairs from my face and accepted the paper. "Is there any coffee?"

"Yes, I'll bring you a cup before I leave. And the doctor is here, too, don't forget." She eyed my sloppy hair and untidy clothing. I didn't care. My fingers trembled as I read the page.

My Dearest Susanna,

Why have you given shelter to our mutual enemy?

It would have been a kindness to let him die when you found him, for if I return to Thorn Hill now I will certainly kill him with my bare hands. It is hard for me to imagine that you would wish such a thing, but it is the truth.

I give you until sundown to remove my cousin from our home. Let us this settle things between us. Make your choice, madam.

—A

I didn't go downstairs.

"Ingrid," I called after my friend, "please send the messenger away. I have no message to give."

With another frown—Ingrid frowned perpetually—she nodded and went downstairs. I went to my room and changed my clothing. I didn't bother with my hair except to pin the strands back away from my face. I planned to have an honest talk with the doctor about Chase's condition and then prepare for Ambrose's arrival. Even if it wasn't today, I needed to know what to do and say when Ambrose did appear. From the tone of his letter, I could see that he assumed I was most pleased to have Chase come to the house, but that was not the truth.

At least not in the beginning.

By the time I dressed, it was a full half hour later. I could hear the doctor's deep booming voice in Chase's room. He was likely cleaning the wound, a painful procedure that required the application of whiskey to the wound to fight any infection. Chase screamed my name, and it was like a dagger shoved in my heart. I practically ran into the room and ordered the doctor out.

"Susanna! Make him stop!" Chase was in tears. I could see that the fever had not yet completely left him, but the pain and was making him crazy. I took the bottle from the doctor and poured a glass of the whiskey for Chase.

"Drink this! Don't sip it. Drink it down. That's good." I filled the glass again, and he drank another shot. I turned to the doctor. "The next time you tend to his wounds, make sure he has taken his medicine first."

"Well, madam," he said, "I suppose whiskey is a kind of medicine. I'll do as you ask, Miss Susanna. My apologies, sir."

Chase nodded once and gritted his teeth as the man probed the wound. The doctor continued, "Good! That looks good! I'd say you have had some good care here, sir. Thank your lucky stars for that. If you'd been shot anywhere else, you might have been left for dead."

Chase closed his eyes and tried to control his breathing. When he opened them again he looked me in my face fully. "And you aren't a dream? You aren't going to disappear? You're not a ghost?"

"No, Chase. I'm not a ghost. I'm a real woman. I'm...I'm still your wife and duty-bound to care for you."

"Susanna, there are things I must say to you." The whiskey had put color back in his cheeks and had loosened his tongue as well.

"Doctor, perhaps you can come back later. Or, if you prefer to stay, which you are welcome to do, you could go down and take some breakfast and coffee. Ingrid has made plenty."

"Oh, that sounds delightful. Thank you, thank you, lady." This was not the doctor who had cared for me, but he was also from the Ramparts and I liked him from the little I knew about him. Once he was gone, Chase grabbed my hands. That frightened me; I hoped he wouldn't tear open his wounds again.

"Kiss me, Susanna. Tell me you have forgiven me. All I could think was to come see you. I don't know what happened to me—I must have been shot when I got out of the carriage that night. How long have I been here?"

"Just a week," I said as I gave him another shot of whiskey.

"I suppose I went mad for a little while. My father told me that you and Ambrose had planned for months to steal our fortune, and at first I didn't believe him. But the night...that night, something within me snapped. I believed him that night, and I was a fool for doing so. I love you, Susanna. I should have known that this was all Ambrose's doing. He hates me beyond reason. He's always hated me. That's why he stole you from me. But then I heard that he was toying with Athena's cousin, Coquette, and I knew he must have tired of you. Whatever passed between us, let it end now. Let it end. I love you, my darling. I am sorry for what I have done to us. I let you spend time with him knowing that he was an evil man. Please, my own love, forgive me. And may our daughter forgive me."

He rambled on and cried, and my heart believed him. It was nine o'clock in the morning; the windows were open for anyone to see us here on the third floor. Sunlight filled the room, and all I could do was cry. I climbed into the bed with him and cried. He held me close and whispered, "My own, Susanna, my darling, my love. I promised to honor and protect you, and I failed you. I listened to my father, and I lost you. Please tell me. I haven't lost you forever, have I?"

I couldn't answer. I could only cry. Chase held me for a long time, and when the door creaked open I didn't care who found us together. All was right in my world once again.

"Miss Susanna, I am leaving for the shop now. Do you need anything? Should I set your tray here?"

"Yes, Ingrid. Thank you." I noticed that she smiled at me, and I smiled back. It was a rare thing to see her smile. "You can send the doctor away too. We don't need him anymore."

"Very well. Rest well, Mister Chase."

He nodded but never took his eyes off me. After she left he whispered, "Are we alone, Susanna?"

"Yes, I think so. There may be a housekeeper downstairs, but she won't come up unless I summon her."

"I scarcely dare to ask what I am about to ask. Make love to me, Susanna. I want to see my wife, to love her, to keep her, to have her. Please don't deny me your love, not one more day. Have mercy on this poor, wretched creature."

I got up and closed the door. He had a serious wound, but I could see that other parts of him worked perfectly, for he'd pulled the cover back to show me his strong body. I locked the door and shed my clothes too. What would it be like to lie with Chase after being with Ambrose for so long? Ambrose knew every curve of my body and knew exactly which ones needed attention. I felt an unexpected twinge of guilt as I walked to the bedside.

But this was my husband, the man I married before God. This could only be right.

"Let me see you, my beauty, my own wife. You'll have to help me, Susanna." Chase's beautiful face held such desire for me that I could not deny him. I would not! For I wanted him too.

"And will you stay with me, Chase? Are you going to cast me off again? I don't think my heart can take such torment again." I lay beside him in the sweaty cotton sheets. The day was warming quickly.

He kissed my forehead softly, and the whiskey on his breath smelled spicy and sweet. I kissed his lips, and in that instant the hardness of my heart faded away. It was gone. I loved Chase Dufresne with all my heart, it was true. What I had with Ambrose had been a dream only.

We are soul mates, Susanna... I seemed to hear him whisper in my ear. I spun about in the bed but saw no one there.

"What is it, love?"

"I thought I heard a voice."

The whiskey made him woozy, and he smiled flirtatiously, "Listen to my voice, my darling. We are one, you and I, just like the priest said. Please make love to me. Let us reconcile in truth, Susanna. I care not what happens tomorrow. I care only about you and me and right now."

And I obeyed him. We made sweet love. We lost ourselves in the beauty of our bodies, and once a desire was sated, another arose. The love we made love was a kind of healing love, and when we were finished we were spent.

"Only once more, my love. Once more. I must feel you again." He'd drunk more whiskey and was feeling no pain now. As our frenzied desire again drew to a conclusion, the door to the room swung open. I could not see who it was; Chase's back was in the way. Then I heard a gunshot, and Chase fell off me and onto the floor in a heap. When the smoke cleared and I stopped screaming, I could see that the bullet had grazed my shoulder and I was covered in my husband's blood.

His murderer stood in the doorway. It was not who I expected at all. It was Chase's right-hand wife, Athena Pelham Dufresne. Her freakishly large eyes stared at me, and they were full of hate.

After a few seconds she put the gun down. The shot never came. She lowered her weapon, then walked over to him and shot him again. Then she turned to me. "I will not kill you, for death is too good for you. Besides, tonight my cousin Coquette will do away with Ambrose Dufresne. He will be dead too. And then we women will be free!" She laughed so hard that she slapped the table under which Chase's body lay. It was then that I noticed she was pregnant. And had been for many months.

"I never want to see your face again, Susanna. Do not come to Sugar Hill, or I will kill you. Just as I killed my unfaithful husband—and yours. You should thank me, you know. All these Dufresne men are devils. Even Ambrose. He would have seduced me too, if I had let him. Told me I was his soul mate, if you can believe that." She waved the gun around as if it were a toy. "Goodbye for the last time, Susanna."

She walked out of the smoke-filled room, glancing at our husband's corpse one last time. When I thought it was safe, I slid down to the floor besides Chase. He was dead. He was most assuredly dead. I curled up beside him and held his body until Nicole finally came upstairs with the sheriff. The next few hours were a mist of despair.

I was shaken from my reverie when Ingrid appeared, back from the shop and terribly upset. "Miss Susanna! We must leave here! The Ramparts are on fire—that madwoman Coquette and her cousin Athena have set the place on fire. They want to kill us all! Grab your bag and let's go! They are evacuating our street." I stepped out on the porch and could see she was telling the truth. The family in the Black House across the street was packing in a mad rush and screaming in fear as the fires inched closer to our street.

"What about Chase? I can't leave his body here."

"Fine, we'll bring him with us, miss, but we have to go."

We raced into the house, and the two of us dragged Chase's body to the carriage, where my driver helped us get him inside. I had my purse, my ledger and not much else. We rode away and left the Ramparts before the fire destroyed everything. Hundreds of men appeared with pails of water, attempting to save the buildings that were already blazing. Grainger drove us deeper into the Ramparts. Didn't he know we had to get away?

"What are you doing?" Ingrid called to him.

"I'm not leaving without Mister Ambrose. It's not far!"

Ingrid began to argue, but I told her to let it go. There had been too much death recently. Too much of everything. I laid Chase's head in my lap and kept him close to me as the carriage banged across knots, stumps and whatever else it could find. Soon we were stopped in front of a house. Grainger hopped down and ran toward the building.

"Oh goodness. This will kill old Grainger. He loves Ambrose like a son." How did I not know that? "He's surely dead, if he's inside there, miss." I got out too. I stood in front of Coquette's house and waited for some sign that Ambrose was safe. None came.

Then I heard him whisper in my ear, "You are my soul mate, Susanna Serene. You always will be." I collapsed on the ground before the little white two-story house that burned. Someone picked me up and put me back in the carriage and rode away to Sugar Hill.

I don't know what I expected to happen, but I didn't expect to find that Athena had abandoned the place, that she'd admitted to her father she had killed her husband. No, I didn't expect that at all. We took Chase inside and laid him out in the dining room. There would be many funerals tomorrow. From what we heard from the servants at Sugar Hill, the fire had all but destroyed the houses on the north end of the road. Thorn Hill alone had survived. But I would never return there. As much as Chase might have wanted me to, I wouldn't. I would never leave his side again. He would lie at rest here, at Sugar Hill. And when I died, I would go with him. At last.

You are my soul mate, Susanna Serene. You belong to me.

I closed the front door and pretended I did not hear him. I closed my heart to him completely. He'd lied to me about a great many things, I soon discovered. I found a plethora of information about Ambrose in Arthur's old desk. For example, I never knew until much later that he had been Chase's half-brother, the son of Arthur and his left-hand wife. And to think, the old man had told the world that his son was his nephew. Shameful. Just for that, I burned his mausoleum the same night the Ramparts burned down.

Nine months later, I gave birth to twin boys; one was blond, with pink skin and a serious nature, and the other had dark, shiny eyes, olive skin and a mouth that never stopped screaming or searching for my breast. It was if the half-brothers were born again, and the thought frightened me. I would raise my sons, Dominick and Champion, to the best of my ability, and I would pray they would become better than their fathers. For I believed with all my heart that I bore a child to each man. Somehow, that had to be true. Their lines continued.

I prayed they would be better men than either.

Epilogue – Jessica

I volunteered to watch the grill while Jamie went in search of more ketchup. He was quiet, pensive, but who could blame him? He'd been under the influence of a determined spirit. It was good of Avery to give him a second chance, but my "sensitivity" told me that they weren't quite right for each other. No. Something wasn't quite right with Jamie. Not just yet.

And it was nice that Avery wanted to have this shindig for us before we rolled out of here in the morning. I lobbied to stay longer, but the Paranormal Channel had somewhere else quite a ways from here for us to explore. I never expected to explore a mine, but apparently that was where we were headed. Some haunted mine up at Ruby Falls in upper Alabama near the Tennessee state line. I hated the idea of leaving here. We'd only scratched the surface of the paranormal activity at Sugar Hill. What had we learned? What had I learned? I learned that there was so much more to paranormal investigation than classifications, shadows and whispers. At the heart of most hauntings there were people, some living and some dead. I hoped I never forgot that, no matter how high our ratings got—and believe me, they were high now.

Jamie gave me a thumbs-up, and I smiled proudly. It was nice to be me again, just plain old me. Not sensitive, psychic me. Just Jessica Chesterfield, plain-Jane girl, chronic doodler and aspiring artist. Jamie took over his spot at the grill, and I pulled my notepad out of my knapsack. I found a nearby bench and began sketching an early blooming azalea bush, but my attention soon shifted to the gazebo. I could see it quite clearly from here. It was old and in need of repair; it looked like it should be torn down, but it was still standing. I was glad to see that.

But I didn't draw it as it was. I drew it as I saw it with my heart. I saw it painted white, the green vines wrapping around the lattice, the faces of stone children poking out from the topiaries. Yes, I could almost imagine being inside the gazebo. I could see the two together, the man and the woman. They both had dark hair, his face handsome and fierce-looking, his full lips longing to kiss hers. I saw her tremble as she removed the pins from her hair. With a look of pure desire, she slid out of her gown and stood before him.

And I sketched. He watched her, wanted her, desired her more than life itself...

My pencil shuffled across the page.

"Jessica! Have you gone deaf? Do you want one or two?"

"What?"

Megan was looking at me like I had two heads. She didn't even notice the sketchbook in my hands. "One hamburger or two? Jamie wants to know."

"Oh. One, please. No mustard." She went off to tell him, and I turned back to my sketch. I stared at it like I'd never seen it before. What had I drawn? Where did that come from? I shook my head and rubbed my fingers over the pictures. Then Avery stood beside me and looked down at the pages.

"You see them too?" she asked.

"Yes, I see them. They haven't left. I wonder if they'll always be here."

She smiled sadly and said nothing else as she examined the page. She touched Ambrose's face with her fingers, and then Reed came to whisper in her ear. She forgot about Ambrose for a moment—that was good. She went with Reed, and they walked down a path to another part of the garden. Jamie didn't appear to notice. He probably should have.

One day she would have to choose. And soon. I wondered if she knew that.

As surely as I knew my own name, I knew I would be back here. I would be back at Sugar Hill. One day, Avery would call me, and I would come back. Somehow, we were connected now. All of us were connected.

"Hello, Handsome," I said to the older man as he slipped quietly into the party through a gap in the hedge. He carried a basket of peaches in his hands. Nobody else seemed to notice him. "Those look like delicious peaches. May I have one?"

"Yes, but just one. These are for Miss Avery. She likes peaches."

I agreed to take just one, and as I reached for it, I listened. It was as if I could hear a radio playing somewhere, an old familiar song.

"You feeling all right?" Concern clouded Handsome's face.

"Must be a radio playing somewhere, 'cause I thought I heard jazz. I think it was Billie Holiday."

Handsome smiled so big I thought his face would split. "You heard her too! Yeah, she's singing. Singing up a storm, like she always does when there's trouble a-brewing."

"Is trouble brewing?"

"Yes, ma'am. There's always trouble brewing these days. But we'll be here. Me and Miss Billie. We'll be here."

"I am glad to hear that, Handsome. And I'll be here too. Whenever I hear the music, I'll come. I'll help."

"You promise? Miss Billie don't sing for everyone. She likes you, though. She sings for you."

"Yes, I'll always come. I will never let her down—or you, Handsome." I dug in my pocket for a business card. This was the first time I'd ever given one away. "Take this. Call me if you hear her singing again and she mentions my name. I want to help you—and Avery. Please call me, Handsome."

"I will, Jessica. I will."

He hugged my neck and handed me an extra peach. We sat on the bench together, eating the juicy peaches and listening to the music. Handsome sang loudly, and soon I was singing with him.

There was no reason to pretend I couldn't hear Billie. Let Mike and Megan think I was crazy. I didn't care. Becker wasn't around; he was undoubtedly saying his goodbyes to Summer Dufresne. No, that couldn't be right. She was over by the grill flirting with Jamie. I wondered where Becker had gone, but I didn't bother to find him. I listened to the music and sang along with Billie.

I wouldn't leave this place for long. Then I had a thought. A true thought. I knew it was true as soon as I thought it.

When I return here, I will never again leave.

It didn't matter. Whatever that meant, it didn't matter because at least I could finally hear the music.

More from M. L. Bullock

From the *Ultimate Seven Sisters Collection*

A smile crept across my face when I turned back to look at the pale faces watching me from behind the lace curtains of the girls' dormitory. I didn't feel sorry for any of them—all of those girls hated me. They thought they were my betters because they were orphans and I was merely the accidental result of my wealthy mother's indiscretion. I couldn't understand why they felt that way. As I told Marie Bettencourt, at least my parents were alive and wealthy. Hers were dead and in the cold, cold ground. "Worm food now, I suppose." Her big dark eyes had swollen with tears, her ugly, fat face contorting as she cried. Mrs. Bedford scolded me for my remarks, but even that did not worry me.

I had a tool much more effective than Mrs. Bedford's threats of letters to the attorney who distributed my allowance or a day without a meal. Mr. Bedford would defend me—for a price. I would have to kiss his thin, dry lips and pretend that he did not peek at my décolletage a little too long. Once he even squeezed my bosom ever so quickly with his rough hands but then pretended it had been an accident. Mr. Bedford never had the courage to lift up my skirt or ask me for a "discreet favor," as my previous chaperone had called it, but I enjoyed making him stare. It had been great fun for a month or two until I saw how easily he could be manipulated.

And now my rescuer had come at last, a man, Louis Beaumont, who claimed to be my mother's brother. I had never met Olivia, my mother. Not that I could re-member, anyway, and I assumed I never would.

Louis Beaumont towered above most men, as tall as an otherworldly prince. He had beautiful blond hair that I wanted to plunge my hands into. It looked like the down of a baby duckling. He had fair skin—so light it almost glowed—with pleasant features, even brows, thick lashes, a manly mouth. It was a shame he was so near a kin because I would have had no objec-tions to whispering "Embrasse-moi" in his ear. Alt-hough I very much doubted Uncle Louis would have indulged my fantasy. How I loved to kiss, and to kiss one so beautiful! That would be heavenly. I had never kissed a handsome man before—I kissed the ice boy once and a farmhand, but neither of them had been handsome or good at kissing.

For three days we traveled in the coach, my uncle ex-plaining what he wanted and how I would benefit if I followed his instructions. According to my uncle, Cousin Calpurnia needed me, or rather, needed a com-panion for the season. The heiress would come out this year, and a certain level of decorum was expected, in-cluding traveling with a suitable companion. "Who would be more suitable than her own cousin?" he asked me with the curl of a smile on his regal face. "Now, dearest Isla," he said, "I am counting on you to be a respectable girl. Leave all that happened before behind in Birmingham—no talking of the Bedfords or anyone else from that life. All will be well now." He patted my hand gently. "We must find Calpurnia a suitable husband, one that will give her the life she's accustomed to and deserves."

Yes, indeed. Now that this Calpurnia needed a proper companion, I had been summoned. I'd never even heard of Miss Calpurnia Cottonwood until now. Where had Uncle Louis been when I ran sobbing in a crumpled dress after falling prey to the lecherous hands of General Harper, my first guardian? Where had he been when I endured the shame and pain of my stolen maidenhead? Where? Was I not Beaumont stock and worthy of rescue? Apparently not. I decided then and there to hate my cousin, no matter how rich she was. Still, I smiled, spreading the skirt of my purple dress neatly around me on the seat. "Yes, Uncle Louis."

"And who knows, ma petite Cherie, perhaps we can find you a good match too. Perhaps a military man or a wealthy merchant. Would you like that?" I gave him another smile and nod before I pretended to be distracted by something out the window. My fate would be in my own hands, that much I knew. Never would I marry. I would make my own future. Calpurnia must be a pitiful, ridiculous kind of girl if she needed my help to land a "suitable" husband with all her affluence.

About the *Ultimate Seven Sisters Collection*

When historian Carrie Jo Jardine accepted her dream job as chief historian at Seven Sisters in Mobile, Alabama, she had no idea what she would encounter. The moldering old plantation housed more than a few boxes of antebellum artifacts and forgotten oil paintings. Secrets lived there—and they demanded to be set free.

This contains the entire supernatural suspense series.

More from M. L. Bullock

From *The Ghosts of Idlewood*

I arrived at Idlewood at seven o'clock thinking I'd have plenty of time to mark the doors with taped signs before the various contractors arrived. There was no electricity, so I wasn't sure what the workmen would actually accomplish today. I'd dressed down this morning in worn blue jeans and a long-sleeved t-shirt. It just felt like that kind of day. The house smelled stale, and it was cool but not freezing. We'd enjoyed a mild February this year, but like they say, "If you don't like the weather in Mobile, just wait a few minutes."

I really hated February. It was "the month of love," and this year I wasn't feeling much like celebrating. I'd given Chip the heave-ho for good right after Christmas, and our friendship hadn't survived the breakup. I hated that because I really did like him as a person, even if he could be narrow-minded about spiritual subjects. I hadn't been seeing anyone, but I was almost ready to get back into the dating game. Almost.

I changed out the batteries in my camera before beginning to document the house. Carrie Jo liked having before, during and after shots of every room.

According to the planning sheet Carrie Jo and I developed last month, all the stage one doors were marked. On her jobs, CJ orchestrated everything: what rooms got painted first, where the computers would go, which room we would store supplies in, that sort of thing. I also put no-entry signs on rooms that weren't safe or were off-limits to curious workers. The home was mostly empty, but there were some pricy mantelpieces and other components that would fetch a fair price if you knew where to unload stolen items such as high-end antiques. Surprisingly, many people did.

I'd start the pictures on the top floor and work my way down. I peeked out the front door quickly to see if CJ was here. No sign of her yet, which wasn't like her at all. She was usually the early bird. I smiled, feeling good that Carrie Jo trusted me enough to give me the keys to this grand old place. There were three floors, although the attic space wasn't a real priority for our project. The windows would be changed, the floors and roof inspected, but not a lot of cosmetic changes were planned for up there beyond that. We'd prepare it for future storage of seasonal decorations and miscellaneous supplies. Seemed a waste to me. I liked the attic; it was roomy, like an amazing loft apartment. But it was no surprise I was drawn to it—when I was a kid, I practically lived in my tree house.

I stuffed my cell phone in my pocket and jogged up the wide staircase in the foyer. I could hear birds chirping upstairs; they probably flew in through a broken window. There were quite a few of them from the sound of it. Since I hadn't labeled any doors upstairs or in the attic, I hadn't had the opportunity to explore much up there. It felt strangely exhilarating to do so all by myself. The first flight of stairs appeared safe, but I took my time on the next two. Water damage wasn't always easy to spot, and I had no desire to fall through a weak floor. When I reached the top of the stairs to the attic, I turned the knob and was surprised to find it locked.

"What?" I twisted it again and leaned against the door this time, but it wouldn't move. I didn't see a keyhole, so that meant it wasn't locked after all. I supposed it was merely stuck, the wood probably swollen from moisture. "Rats," I said. I set my jaw and tried one last time. The third time must have been the charm because it opened freely, as if it hadn't given me a world of problems before. I nearly fell as it gave way, laughing at myself as I regained my balance quickly. I reached for my camera and flipped it to the video setting. I panned the room to record the contents. There were quite a few old trunks, boxes and even the obligatory dressmaker's dummy. It was a nerd girl historian's dream come true.

Like an amateur documentarian, I spoke to the camera: "Maiden voyage into the attic at Idlewood. Today is February 4th. This is Rachel Kowalski recording."

Rachel Kowalski recording, something whispered back. My back straightened, and the fine hairs on my arms lifted as if to alert me to the presence of someone or something unseen.

I froze and said, "Hello?" I was happy to hear my voice and my voice alone echo back to me.

Hello?

About *The Ghosts of Idlewood*

When a team of historians takes on the task of restoring the Idlewood plantation to its former glory, they discover there's more to the moldering old home than meets the eye. The long-dead Ferguson children don't seem to know they're dead. A mysterious clock, a devilish fog and the Shadow Man add to the supernatural tension that begins to build in the house. Lead historian Carrie Jo Stuart and her assistant Rachel must use their special abilities to get to the bottom of the many mysteries that the house holds.

Detra Ann and Henri get a reality check, of the supernatural kind, and Deidre Jardine finally comes face to face with the past.

More from M. L. Bullock

From *The Tale of Nefret*

Clapping my hands three times, I smiled, amused at the half-dozen pairs of dark eyes that watched me entranced with every word and movement I made. "And then she crept up to the rock door and clapped her hands again..." *Clap, clap, clap.* The children squealed with delight as I weaved my story. This was one of their favorites, The Story of Mahara, about an adventurous queen who constantly fought magical creatures to win back her clan's stolen treasures.

"Mahara crouched down as low as she could." I demonstrated, squatting as low as I could in the tent. "She knew that the serpent could only see her if she stood up tall, for he had very poor eyesight. If she was going to steal back the jewel, she would have to crawl her way into the den, just as the serpent opened the door. She was terrified, but the words of her mother rang in her ears: 'Please, Mahara! Bring back our treasures and restore our honor!'"

I crawled around, pretending to be Mahara. The children giggled. "Now Mahara had to be very quiet. The bones of a hundred warriors lay in the serpent's cave. One wrong move and that old snake would see her and...catch her!" I grabbed at a nearby child, who screamed in surprise. Before I could finish my tale, Pah entered our tent, a look of disgust on her face.

"What is this? Must our tent now become a play-ground? Out! All of you, out! Today is a special day, and we have to get ready."

The children complained loudly, "We want to hear Nefret's story! Can't we stay a little longer?"

Pah shook her head, and her long, straight hair shimmered. "Out! Now!" she scolded the spokesman for the group.

"Run along. There will be time for stories later," I promised them.

As the heavy curtain fell behind them, I gave Pah an unhappy look. She simply shook her head. "You shouldn't make promises that you may not be able to keep, Nefret. You do not know what the future holds."

"Why must you treat them so? They are only chil-dren!" I set about dressing for the day. Today we were to dress simply with an aba—a sleeveless coat and trousers. I chose green as my color, and Pah wore blue. I cinched the aba at the waist with a thick leather belt. I wore my hair in a long braid. My fin-gers trembled as I cinched it with a small bit of cloth.

"Well, if nothing else, you'll be queen of the children, Nefret."

About *The Tale of Nefret*

Twin daughters of an ancient Bedouin king struggle under the weight of an ominous prophecy that threatens to divide them forever. Royal sibling rivalry explodes as the young women realize that they must fight for their future and for the love of Alexio, the man they both love. *The Tale of Nefret* chronicles their lives as they travel in two different directions. One sister becomes the leader of the Meshwesh while the other travels to Egypt as an unwilling gift to Pharaoh.

More from M. L. Bullock

From *The Mermaid's Gift*

Dauphin Island had more than its share of weirdness—a fact illustrated by tomorrow's Mullet Toss—but it was home to me. It wasn't as popular as nearby Sand Island or Frenchman Bay, and we islanders clung to our small-town identity like it was a badge of honor. Almost unanimously, islanders refused to succumb to the pressure of beach developers and big-city politicians who occasionally visited our pristine stretches of sand with dollar signs in their eyes. No matter how they sweet-talked the town elders, they left unsatisfied time and time again, with the exception of a lone tower of condominiums that stood awkwardly in the center of the island. As someone said recently at our monthly town meeting, "We don't need all that hoopla." That seemed to be the general sense of things, and although I valued what they were trying to preserve, I didn't always agree with my fellow business owners and residents. Still, I was just Nike Augustine, the girl with a weird name and a love for french fries but most notably the granddaughter of the late Jack Augustine, respected one-time mayor of Dauphin Island. What did I know? I was too young to appreciate the importance of protecting our sheltered island. Or so I had been told. So island folk such as myself made the bulk of our money during spring break and the Deep Sea Fishing Rodeo in July. It was enough to make a girl nuts.

But despite this prime example of narrow-mindedness, I fit in here. Along with all the oddities like the island clock that never worked properly, the abandoned lighthouse that everyone believed was haunted and the fake purple shark that hung outside my grandfather's souvenir shop. I reminded myself of that when the overwhelming desire to wander over-took me, as it threatened to do today and had done most days recently. I had even begun to dream of diving into the ocean and swimming as far down as I could. Pretty crazy since I feared the water, or more specifically what swam hidden in the darkness. An-other Nike eccentricity. Only my grandfather under-stood my reluctance, but he was no longer here to tell me I wasn't crazy. My fear of water separated me from my friends, who practically lived in or on the waters of the Gulf of Mexico or the Mobile Bay most of the year.

Meandering down the aisles of the souvenir shop, I stopped occasionally to turn a glass dolphin and rear-range a few baskets of dusty shells. I halfheartedly slapped the shelves with my dust rag and glanced at the clock again and again until finally the shark-tooth-tipped hands hit five o'clock. With a bored sigh, I walked to the door, turned the sign to Closed and flicked off the neon sign that glowed: "Shipwreck Souvenirs." I'd keep longer hours when spring break began, but for now it was 9 to 5.

I walked to the storeroom to retrieve the straw broom. I had to pay homage to tradition and make a quick pass over the chipped floor. I'd had barely any traffic today, just a few landlubbers hoping to avoid the spring breakers; as many early birds had discovered, the cold Gulf waters weren't warm enough to frolic in yet. Probably fewer than a dozen people had darkened my door today, and only half of those had the courtesy to buy something. With another sigh, I remembered the annoying child who had rubbed his sticky hands all over the inflatables before announcing to the world that he had to pee. I thanked my Lucky Stars that I didn't have kids. But then again, I would need a boyfriend or husband for that, right?

Oh, yeah. I get to clean the toilets, too.

I wondered what the little miscreant had left behind for me in the tiny bathroom. No sense in griping about it. It was me or no one. I wouldn't be hiring any help anytime soon. I grabbed the broom and turned to take care of the task at hand when I heard a suspicious sound that made me pause.

Someone was near the back door, rattling through the garbage cans. I could hear the metal lid banging on the ground. Might be a cat or dog, but it might also be Dauphin Island's latest homeless resident. We had a few, but this lost soul tugged at my heartstrings. I had never seen a woman without a place to live. So far she had refused to tell me her name or speak to me at all. Perhaps she was hard of hearing too? Whatever the case, it sounded as if she weren't above digging through my trash cans. Which meant even more work for me. "Hey," I called through the door, hoping to stop her before she destroyed it.

I had remembered her today as I was eating my lunch. I saved her half of my club sandwich. I had hoped I could tempt her to talk to me, but as if she knew what I had planned, she'd made herself scarce. Until now.

I slung the door open, and the blinds crashed into the mauve-painted wall. Nobody was there, but a torn bag of trash lay on the ground. I yelled in the direction of the cans, "Hey! You don't have to tear up the garbage! I have food for you. Are you hungry?"

I might as well have been talking to the dolphins that splashed offshore. Nobody answered me. "I know you're there! I just heard you in my trash. Come out, lady. I won't hurt you." Still nobody answered. I heard a sound like a low growl coming from the side of my store.

What the heck was that?

Immediately I felt my adrenaline surge. Danger stalked close. I ran to the back wall of my shop and flattened myself against the rough wood. I heard the growl again. Was that a possum? Gator? Rabies-crazed homeless lady? I knew I shouldn't have started binge-watching *The Walking Dead* this week. There was absolutely nothing wrong with my imagination. My mind reeled with the possibilities. After a few seconds I quietly reasoned with myself. I didn't have time for this. Time to face the beast—whatever it might be.

About *The Mermaid's Gift*

Nike Augustine isn't your average girl next door. She's a spunky siren but, thanks to a memory loss, doesn't know it—yet. By day, she runs a souvenir shop on Dauphin Island off the coast of Alabama, but a chance encounter opens her eyes to the supernatural creatures that call the island home, including a mermaid, a fallen goddess and a host of other beings. When an old enemy appears and attempts to breach the Sirens Gate, Nike and her friends must take to the water to prevent the resurrection of a long-dead relative...but the cost might be too high.

To make matters worse, Nike has to choose between longtime crush, Officer Cruise Castille and Ramara, a handsome supernaturate who has proven he's willing to lose everything—including his powers—for the woman he loves.

Read more from M.L. Bullock

The Seven Sisters Series

Seven Sisters
Moonlight Falls on Seven Sisters
Shadows Stir at Seven Sisters
The Stars that Fell
The Stars We Walked Upon
The Sun Rises Over Seven Sisters

The Idlewood Series

The Ghosts of Idlewood
Dreams of Idlewood
The Whispering Saint
The Haunted Child

Return to Seven Sisters
(A Seven Sisters Sequel Series)

The Roses of Mobile
A Garden of Thorns (forthcoming)
All the Summer Roses (forthcoming)
Blooms Torn Asunder (forthcoming)
A Wreath of Roses (forthcoming)

Beyond Seven Sisters
(A Forthcoming Seven Sisters Spin-Off Series)

Beyond Seven Sisters
Keeper of My Heart
The Island Rose

Cotton City Antiques
(A Forthcoming Seven Sisters Spin-Off Series)

A Voice from Her Past
The Haunted Letter
Henri's Ghost Light
Missing Time in Mobile
Phantom Photos of Tomorrow
The Weeping of Angels

The Gulf Coast Paranormal Series

The Ghosts of Kali Oka Road
The Ghosts of the Crescent Theater
A Haunting on Bloodgood Row
The Legend of the Ghost Queen
A Haunting at Dixie House (forthcoming)
The Ghost Lights of Forrest Field (forthcoming)
The Ghost of Gabrielle Bonet (forthcoming)
The Ghosts of Harrington Farms (forthcoming)
The Creature on Crenshaw Road (forthcoming)

Storm Castle Series (forthcoming)

The Haunting of Joanna Storm
The Disappearance of Joanna Storm
The Ghost of Joanna Storm

To receive updates on her latest releases,
visit her website at MLBullock.com
and subscribe to her mailing list.

About the Author

Author of the best-selling *Seven Sisters* series and the *Desert Queen* series, M.L. Bullock has been storytelling since she was a child. A student of archaeology, she loves weaving stories that feature her favorite historical characters—including Nefertiti. She currently lives on the Gulf Coast with her family but travels frequently to exotic locations around the globe.

Made in the USA
Coppell, TX
11 December 2020